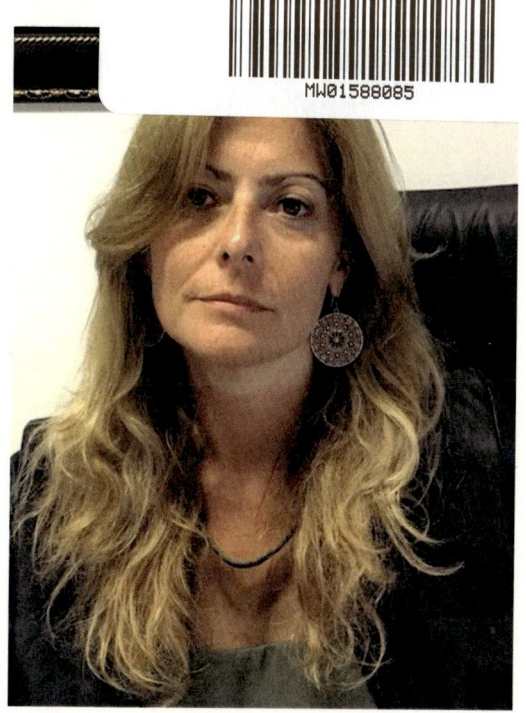

About the Author

Laura Guercio is a lawyer and a professor of international relations at the University Cusano in Rome. She holds a degree in law, political science and international relations with a PhD in Social Science. For many years, she has been engaged in the field of human rights. Formerly a member of the Management Board of the EU Fundamental Rights Agency and Secretary General of the Inter-ministerial Committee for Human Rights at the Italian Ministry of Foreign Affairs, she is currently the Secretary General of the Universities Network for Children in Armed Conflict. She is involved in numerous international projects for the promotion of fundamental rights in the MENA region, Africa and Asia.

The Roses of Agbogbloshie

Laura Guercio

The Roses of Agbogbloshie

Olympia Publishers
London

www.olympiapublishers.com
OLYMPIA PAPERBACK EDITION

Copyright © Laura Guercio 2025

The right of Laura Guercio to be identified as author of this work has been asserted in accordance with sections 77 and 78 of the Copyright, Designs and Patents Act 1988.

All Rights Reserved

No reproduction, copy or transmission of this publication may be made without written permission.
No paragraph of this publication may be reproduced, copied or transmitted save with the written permission of the publisher, or in accordance with the provisions of the Copyright Act 1956 (as amended).

Any person who commits any unauthorised act in relation to this publication may be liable to criminal prosecution and civil claims for damage.

A CIP catalogue record for this title is available from the British Library.

ISBN: 978-1-83543-346-1

This is a work of fiction.
Names, characters, places and incidents originate from the writer's imagination. Any resemblance to actual persons, living or dead, is purely coincidental.

First Published in 2025

Olympia Publishers
Tallis House
2 Tallis Street
London
EC4Y 0AB

Printed in Great Britain

Dedication

To all those I have met in my life.

INTRODUCTION

There is a suburb to the northwest of the city of Accra, located on the banks of the Korle Lagoon, not far from the Port of Tema. Not everyone in Ghana, and very few people in the world, know its name, Agbogbloshie. Anyone who knows anything about it knows that it is also called 'Sodom and Gomorrah'.

This is not merely due to the rampant crime and the difficult conditions in which the inhabitants of the houses and shacks live, piled up in the mud and dirt. There is something else that makes Agbogbloshie different from many other sad realities of poverty and abandonment spread across Africa and beyond. Millions of people from richer parts of the world, most of them without knowing it, send something personal here; an object or a tool that served for some time to make their and our lives easier and more comfortable.

Agbogbloshie is a huge electronic and technological waste dump. Every day, hundreds of tons of monitors, computers, keyboards, cathode ray tubes, video recorders and other component parts pour into it. Once instruments of well-being, they are now reduced to a mass of metal, which is often poisonous and is devastating for the environment and for living beings.

Thousands of people spend their lives here, rummaging with their bare hands and without any protection among that rubbish, desperate to get something else out of it, for example, copper from the electric wires which they burn to eliminate the plastic casings. Most of these are children who work their way through and play in the vast expanse of waste, while they never stop dreaming.

This story is about the children of Agbogbloshie.

London, December 3
To the Dean of the Faculty of Medicine

Dear Dean,

I have just returned from Accra, where I carried out my internship, agreed with your research institute abroad, near the gigantic Agbogbloshie technological waste dump, studying the effects of contact with this waste on the human body. My work on landfill poisoning has focused on the consequences for children, and I am now preparing to present and explain my report during the specialisation exam, in the next few days.

I will not dwell here on the data in my report. I limit myself to repeating that the effects of contact with technological waste are devastating. In fact, I write this letter to thank you and your institute for the opportunity you have given me to carry out my research directly in the field. By 'field' I mean a place totally devastated by the storage and disposal of waste.

Thank you for an experience that I consider, without rhetoric, to be decisive in my career, not only professionally but in human terms.

Thousands of people spend hours and hours among electronic waste, WEEE material or, what is called, 'e-waste' in the Agbogbloshie landfill. Rich and industrialised countries send this waste, often under the cover of donations of machinery or development aid, knowing full well that it consists mostly of technologically outdated and obsolete components or simply unusable material.

Even these materials represent a small source of wealth for those who live in Agbogbloshie: the most desperate children of Ghana. Thousands of people pass their days in the landfill, burning the plastic from electronic machines so they can recover the copper and aluminium.

They then deliver them to 'recuperators', the first step in the hierarchy of an organisation that de facto dominates the area, devoid of any real control or intervention by state institutions.

The recuperators pay the equivalent of a couple of dollars for every five kilos of material collected with the bare hands of people in close contact with the fumes of the fires and poisonous metals such as lead, barium and mercury.

Many are children, unaware of the enormous risks. I kept eight of these children under constant medical monitoring for five months. All now have very serious and, unfortunately, irreversible pathologies, by any reasonable clinical evaluation. Two have kidney dysfunction; three presents with forms of stomach cancer, one case now in an advanced state; and the other three have serious respiratory problems.

But I'm not writing just about clinical data. And I'm not looking for an outpouring of emotion or a mere denunciation. You embody an institution dedicated to research, the deepest sense of the university experience. I believe that in our field, the greatest danger of betraying this sense is forgetting the person and considering only the disease. And unfortunately, it happens often.

I don't want that to happen now, so I'm telling you the names of the children: Kofi, Ama, Martin, Nelson, Aziz, Kwame known as Palletta, Nii and Osagyefo.

They all have beautiful faces and lively eyes. Like all

children, they want to play, listen to music, hear fairy tales and the stories of their ancestors, eat candies when they are given them, and collect coloured cards. If you ask them what they want to be when they grow up, they all have a dream of achievement.

I tell you, and even more I tell myself, all of this with the conviction that the experience at Agbogbloshie, offered to me by the Institute, has inoculated me from the danger of forgetting the people.

After these five months, I know clearly that I really need to feel like a doctor, to feel like a person who manages to be moved and horrified and who can cry in front of the sufferings of innocents. But perhaps even more, I need to find arguments and the determination to distinguish myself from our rich world, which has thrown these children and so many others like them into a life without a future, has made them human trash among the electronic trash.

I repeat again that I am grateful to the Institute. But I still can't help wondering about what seems to me to be schizophrenia. So I ask you too: isn't it problematic that many of the computers in these landfills may also have come from our Institute, which then sends one of its specialists to study the devastating effects?

In the next few days, I will discuss my research and finish my graduate course. Then I will practice the profession I have always wanted. But right now, what I hope for the most is never to forget the faces of those children and, above all, never to forget the complex feelings that filled – and wounded – my spirit.

Maybe my generation is already too compromised by now, and maybe we won't be able to get out of this vicious circle that, hypocritically, leads us to be 'missionaries' in places we have destroyed – or, worse still, to forget them. But I still want to believe that there might be something other than all of this. As I have written, this letter is more for me than for you, so that tomorrow, when I work on disease, I can stop and look into the eyes of patients without shame.

I thank you again for the opportunity that you and your institute have given me and I hope I will not betray the trust placed in me. I conclude by informing you that I am returning the computer that was given to me by the Institute now that I have a replacement.

Best regards,
Catherine Miller

London, December 4

"Good morning to all of you dear listener friends, from your favourite radio station. Got coffee? Took a shower? Do you still need to wake up? So stay with us on Radio WFY for your daily charge for a great day. I'm Nigel Tornton, here for you, to brighten your morning and electrify your day... and *brrr...* watch out! It's cold out there, guys.

"In here we are a revolution of warmth and passion. We want to change the world, paint everything black to erase everything that afflicts us and obscures the light that burns within us... and here it is... *Paint it Black!*"

There wasn't a day that Nigel didn't play a track from his beloved Rolling Stones. He had grown up with their songs. The British band's records had held an important place among the many in his home, a house where there was sheet music in practically every room. His violinist mother and his flautist father had nourished his childhood and adolescence with music – not only classical music, such as the masterpieces of Bach and Mozart, but also the best of Simon & Garfunkel, the Beatles or the Rolling Stones, expressions of a world they lived and believed in.

As a child, Nigel spent hours listening to the harmonious sequence of notes produced by the bow as his mother's long thin hands moved on the strings of the violin. He observed the elegant shape of this woman who became one with that small wooden box from which she drew a sound that was sometimes frantic, sometimes very sweet, sometimes cheerful, and sometimes as poignant as a crying human voice.

On the few occasions that he had approached his mother's violin in secret, he had tried in vain to understand how that sound was born by rubbing horsehair on strings – as they had explained to him.

In the late 1960s, those sounds and that image had fascinated a young flautist, also a student at the Royal Academy of Music, who later became a colleague in the London Symphony Orchestra. The two shared their passion, where each instrument is like a soul that speaks to others and harmonises in one incredible voice. They had found love and married without waiting too long, becoming parents immediately with the arrival of Nigel. Music became the constant companion of this child, a continuous, enveloping experience that taught him to listen to and understand the rhythms of his own emotions. Among the best memories of his childhood were concerts staged in the evening intimacy of the family home where Nigel was silent and the only spectator, enraptured each time by the magical sound of a piece of wood in the shape of an amphora and that long tube full of holes that transformed his father's voice into musical notes.

Paint it Black was reaching its last notes when Rebecca, the program assistant, placed a Post-it note on the window of the soundproof room. A few words alarmed him: *"The boss wants to talk to you after the transmission."*

"Trouble ahead," he thought. The radio station was going through a period of hardship, and it was likely that the director wanted to announce Nigel's dismissal or at least a salary cut.

Thank goodness he owned a house. Judith, his partner of six years, was a nurse and earned more than he did, and they had no children. In the worst-case scenario, they still could hold up. He put those thoughts aside as soon as the song ended.

"Did you like that, guys? How can we not be moved by this song composed by The Rolling Stones in 1966, which is still today a piece that enters our veins, our blood and makes us vibrate? In 2004 it reached a hundred and seventy-six in the list of the best five hundred songs ever, compiled by *Rolling Stone magazine*, and that list contains no fewer than fourteen other songs by the band. Only another band surpasses them, one that has marked the lives of all of us, of those who have had the good fortune to listen to them live and of those who, like me, have only heard them on records or in films. So this is for you: piano, guitar, electric and percussion bass, as well as violins, viola, cellos, contra bass flute; all this to accompany one of the most famous choral lines... 'Take a sad song and make it better... Hey Jude don't be afraid...' Hey kids, never be afraid."

Hey Jude by the Beatles was the song Nigel had listened to most often in his childhood. Dad never tired of singing it and acclaiming it as a triumph of pop music, a masterpiece enclosed in seven minutes and eleven seconds, an exceptional duration for a single. Nigel had always thought that it deserved more than eighth place in the Rolling Stone ranking but was well aware that his judgment was influenced by his father's preferences and the speeches in those evenings his parents organised at home with their friends.

Since he was a child, Nigel had been allowed to take part and dine with his parents and listen to their discussions. For the Torntons, it was a way of educating their son. For Nigel, it was a source of pride to be with adults and absorb their thoughts, only to contest them later as a teenager. He remembered how his parents' calm often gave way to a feverish fervour on those evenings as, very often, discussions arose about concepts and places that were still unclear to him, such as war, revolution, pacifism, Vietnam, Laos and Cambodia. He would listen until he fell asleep and his mother would take him in her arms to take him to bed. Later he realised that the thing that made the greatest impression on him was the sense of restlessness of all those young people who were uncomfortable in the world they had found and were determined to turn it upside down and make it better, but without succeeding.

Many of those idealistic young people just settled down, and this was the main accusation that Nigel made against his parents and their generation. For him, the Rolling Stones' *Paint it Black* remained the anthem of an unfinished battle. Failure had also generated a sort of apathy in those people – and Nigel was one of them – who were unable to build anything real and positive on it.

However, he knew that he wasn't better at this than his parents: they hadn't won their battle, but at least they had tried, they had fought; he had never even started. But he loved the music of those years because of this too: it was a sort of nostalgia for a future he had never begun to commit to. His radio show, on air every morning from seven to eight, was a tribute to the past but also to a tomorrow in which he would like to believe now, as his parents had believed at the time.

"Hey guys, are you still tuned in?" he resumed as soon as the song ended. "Are you already running down the street to get to work? If you're in line in your car, let's stop for a moment to think. But what should we be afraid of? *Hey Jude*, for a moment it's you. Call in! I'm here with you this morning to talk together about what scares us most, a cat crossing our street, the neighbour we don't know well, the job we could lose. I'm here to share with all of you... Hello who am I talking to?"

A woman's voice answered. The format of Nigel's broadcast was the usual tried and tested way of alternating the musical pieces with short live interventions from the listeners. He was good at grasping the essence of what his interlocutors proposed and respected the fast radio rhythms. His audience and approval ratings were not very high, and he hoped that the manager wanted to talk to him about a pay cut and not about a layoff.

Maybe two minutes went by between closing the show and Nigel's knock on his boss's door.

"Come in, Nigel," boomed Mike, who was a tall, corpulent man with a round face, made pleasant by two red cheeks which he attributed to a circulation problem and others assumed was due to a certain predilection for wine and spirits.

"Hi, Mike, they told me you wanted to talk to me."

"Yes, take a seat; a matter of a minute."

Nigel didn't know whether to relax or worry further at this joke. Usually, it was a matter of a minute to hear, "You're fired." And if you wanted to sweeten the pill with speeches like, "You are an important element for this company, and we will never forget you," three minutes in all.

"I thought I'd charge you with a report for Margaret, who was interested in this, but she has just given birth, so we won't see her at work for a while."

"Oh, I didn't know. Did she have a boy or a girl?"

"It doesn't surprise me she didn't tell you. I don't think there's good blood between you." As brusque as Mike was, he was far more sensitive and attentive than he showed. "Anyway, she's fine and has had a four-kilo girl. Not bad considering she's an anchovy. I still can't figure out where that brat was being held. But let's get back to the point. Given the mess these days with the streets full of rubbish, I want you to do a report on the failure to collect rubbish. Data, people's criticisms, interviews with the heads of the institutions involved; you will spend five minutes of your broadcast on it. Expected day: December 11."

"Me? But boss, I deal with music! At most, I can give you a

review on the chimney sweep song in *Mary Poppins*!" Nigel immediately noticed that Mike didn't like that joke, but he reiterated the concept: "What do I know about these things? And it's not the trend of my space!"

"Until now. But starting today I want your space to have information on politics, administration and social problems too... You go on the air from seven to eight. At that time on other stations, there are programs with space for debate and information. People are already wide awake, eager to get to work and to know what is happening in our city and in the world."

"Are there any share issues I'm not aware of?"

"No, no drop. But we have to renew ourselves. In the meantime, you cover this topic and then we'll think about the next ones."

"But I don't know anything about rubbish... Besides, Mike, we should discuss it first at the next editorial meeting. It's not really the way we do things."

"Nigel," Mike accentuated the name looking into his eyes. "First, I'm giving you the luxury of five days, all the time necessary to do a five-minute piece that a rookie could put together in twenty-four hours. I'm giving you this time, because on December 11 the London Assembly publishes its findings on the recent waste collection inefficiencies. Second, have you ever seen me hold back for things which 'aren't quite the way we do things'? Get lost! And start working on it. Here's the file of material Margaret collected. Take it, study, prepare and disappear. On the 11th I want to hear your report on the fucking trash. Have I been clear enough?"

Mike picked up a small blue booklet from the papers on his desk and handed it to Nigel who nodded and walked out of the room, annoyed and reassured in equal measure.

Agbogbloshie, November 23

The curtain that separated the Kwabla siblings' bed from their parents', and from the rest of what was the only room in the house, opened slowly and let in the harsh but low light of a gas lamp burning on a wooden table on the opposite wall as a tall, slender figure entered in silence.

The woman bent over the three children, watching their breathing for fear of recognising in them the hint of the rattle that every night she heard from her husband who slept next to her and which she knew was also hers. But the children slept well, and for an instant she was reassured, even if she knew the truth.

She knew of the poisoned air, water and earth in the place that was now her home, in the place where her family's flight from the north of the country had ended years before, exhausted by drought and tribal strife. And she knew that waking them so early served to give them hope and a defence. And she was saddened by thinking that the price was to take away from them an hour of that sleep which was also a defence.

There is nothing more tender and sweeter than the sleep of children. Their eyes closed in the embrace of their eyelids, perhaps seeing enchanted images, maybe flowers in a sunny meadow, maybe elves and animals dancing and playing in the forest, maybe bodies of water full of fish and lake plants. No one knows the secrets of that nocturnal world, the hidden desires that sleep keeps and protects from memory and from the light of day, and sometimes the bearer of cruel truths.

Even the dreams of the Kwabla siblings, asleep in a single

bed under a blanket of coarse cotton fabric, were precious little caskets of the mystery of the night. From the small window on one side of their bed, the moonlight filtered through to caress the few, poor pieces of furniture in that piece of room beyond the curtain: a small plastic wardrobe, three chairs, also plastic, covered with the children's clothes.

Beyond the curtain was their parents' bed, already empty at that hour, and a slightly larger wooden wardrobe. Another longer curtain closed off the sleeping space from the rest of the house, a large room with a long wooden box the same size as the table, three wooden chairs and two more plastic ones. On one side, there was a small tin kitchen with two burners fed by gas from a cylinder, and three large cans of precious drinking water, cleaner than that in a large chest in the courtyard behind the house, which was used for washing and to water the small garden.

The whole household slept here at night, breakfasted in the morning, and gathered in the evening for dinner based on the eternal fufu, cassava polenta and potato yam to accompany a little meat, when there was some, but more often fish.

Their father brought fish home after he and his workmates had delivered their boat's catch to the market, a haul that was less abundant every month. hat smell of fish was the only sign that distinguished the Kwabla home from the other houses in the confusing agglomeration of wooden or concrete houses and small enclosures – where you could glimpse several cows and a few goats (but no pigs) – in that district.

Agbogbloshie was an ancient fishing village on the Korle Lagoon, where immigration from the north had made it a sort of Muslim enclave of Christian Accra, the capital of Ghana, once the country of gold and cocoa. Now tens of thousands of people were crammed in, right next to the world's largest technological waste dump. The landfill loomed over their lives and somehow made them possible.

The day was marked by the constant noise of the road towards the Port of Tema, and then on towards Accra. But in the depths of the night, the road was silent and the only reminder of the obsessive presence of the landfill was the pungent and persistent smell of burnt plastic. Everything else was motionless, muffled.

At this time, the little land wind that rippled the shores of the Gulf of Guinea in the months without the monsoon had not yet risen. Not a single branch moved from the few plane, mahogany and cedar trees that survived among the cluster of houses built around the old canals which were now reduced to open-air sewers. And the only masters of that desolation at that hour were a few stray dogs and cats that loitered in the narrow lanes of dusty earth.

The woman brought her face close to that of the older boy, touched his cheek with her lips, and pronounced his name softly: "Kofi, Kofi." She stroked his thick, curly hair. She continued saying his name until the child began to contort his face, rub his eyes and stretch his legs and his small, slender arms.

Still dazed, Kofi looked up at his mother's face and smiled back. There is no child who does not want to be woken up by the reassuring voice and a caress from of his mother. Abenà understood this as a child and had promised herself to give it to her children every morning. She had only three children because all her subsequent pregnancies had ended in miscarriages, thorns that she carried in her heart. She drove the thought away and began to sing the first notes of an English song that always accompanied her little ones as they fell asleep and when they woke. It was a song she had heard from a tape, played in the big black jeep of a German gentleman who had visited on behalf of an important foreign organisation which he defined as 'a humanitarian association'.

The children had never understood what he meant by 'humanitarian' or what this gentleman who played the music of an English group called 'cockroaches' (The Beatles) actually did. The name of those insects, which mothers always feared could settle in houses, made them laugh. But apart from the intriguing name, what captivated the children was the music, sometimes melodic, sometimes rock, the songs they learned to sing and to whose sudden notes they danced.

Abenà's children were particularly impressed by the song now sung by their mother: "Let me take you down,

'Cause I'm going to Strawberry Fields,

Nothing is real,

And nothing to get hung about,

Strawberry Fields forever..."

The image of that field of red, sweet and juicy strawberries had been explained by Father Angelo, their main adult friend, the rector and the soul of the complex that functioned as a school and social centre as well as a church for the very few Catholics of Agbogbloshie. The complex was also frequented by many Muslims, not just children, in a climate of mutual friendship and solidarity stronger than any attempt, however rare in Agbogbloshie, at radical religious indoctrination. The centre also practically had a regulation clay soccer field as its flagship. According to Father Angelo, strawberries were used to make the red candies they liked so much, which were sweeter than mangoes or pineapples, and the children fantasised about playing in a field like this, away from the dust and metal of their landfill one day.

"Wake up, honey, it's time to get ready."

Slowly, Kofi began to lift his body from the bed, and then, with a sudden gesture, he threw himself into his mother's embrace, closing his eyes for a few more moments in that refuge.

Abenà stroked his hair again and gave him a snapping kiss on the head.

"Come on, darling, get ready. Now I'm going to wake up your sister too."

She walked around the bed and approached Kofi's little sister, who was hugging a woollen donkey with a red cloth cap, which never left her side during the night.

With the same sweetness, Abenà kissed Ama's forehead and pronounced her name, until the little girl first began to fidget, annoyed, and then she, too, stretched her thin arms and slender legs from their bony knees.

"Mum... I'm sleepy. I want to sleep again."

Abenà sang the song of the strawberry field, to which the little girl often invented dance movements which were very different from those danced to the sound of traditional community songs.

Ama squeezed her little donkey even tighter, closing her eyes.

"Love up, wake up. And now."

"Already? But I'm still sleepy, Mum... and my little donkey too."

By now Kofi was already dressed in the trousers that Abenà had folded the night before and the Bayern football team shirt that he had received as a gift from the elegant gentleman from the 'humanitarian association'.

"Come on, Ama," she said decisively, "the sorceress is waiting for us."

"Okay, okay. I'm getting up now!" The little girl huffed, and still dazed from sleep, she put on her Havana weekday dress and a pair of sneakers with pink laces. She combed her hair and then turned to her mother to make her two braids that descended on either side of her lively little face.

"Do you know, Mum, that yesterday, Gugu asked me to give her my shoes? She said she didn't have any. But I told her that I couldn't give them to her because they have laces which are my favourite."

"You did well. You know that Father Angelo gave us the right to avoid walking barefoot."

"But why don't Gugu and other children have shoes like us, Mother?"

"Father Angelo said that all your other friends will soon have them too. So if Gugu asks for yours again, tell her that soon she too will be walking in her shoes."

"Yes, Mum, and then I promised Samia I'd give them to her when she gets older. She likes pink too, like me. Look how she's still sleeping, Mother."

The youngest of Abenà's children continued to sleep peacefully in the centre of the pallet which by now had become everything to her, and her mother arranged the blanket better for her.

From the small window they could see the moon silhouetted in the darkness. They had always imagined her as a living presence, showing every month the smiling face of a fat woman who maternally watched over all the children. They scrutinised her deeply, trying to catch her eyes hidden by her own brightness and which, they were sure, would follow them for the whole road they were about to travel.

Abenà called them back.

"Children, you must go now, or else you will be late."

"Mum, I'm still sleepy!" Kofi lamented to Abenà.

"I know, but after this week you won't have to wake up so early again."

"What does that mean? That it will all be over in a week?" Kofi asked.

"Yes, one more week and that's it. But go now, otherwise you'll be late this time too," Abenà said in a decisive tone, greeting Ama with another snapping kiss and Kofi with a pat on the head and the usual fluff of the hair that the boy adored.

London, December 4

Judith's comment when he called to tell her the news was reassuring. "Well, at least it gives a new look to your program. It was time. You couldn't just keep talking about music, Nigel. You've continued to complain about what doesn't work in society and the failures of those who have preceded us, for years. Now you have the opportunity to talk about it with your broadcast and to let all your listeners know what you think. Don't you think it's an important opportunity for someone who does your job and wants real contact with their audience?"

She was right. Most of the time, Nigel envied her ability to have a global view of things, without ever being held up by details. They had met in the hospital, where he had undergone emergency surgery for the removal of a flaring appendix, and the nurse had continued to care for him even after he was released from the hospital. She hadn't stopped since. It was the Hemingway story, they always commented, but without the final tears. They had never really talked about marriage, or if they had, they had concluded that it made no sense, except as a legacy of beliefs and formal guarantees valid for a society that no longer existed.

If this was really the reason for not questioning what they had, or if it was instead just an excuse, they didn't stop to think about it much; they were fine as they were, and the rest didn't matter. Once, they had abruptly ended a discussion with a couple of friends who had based their happiness on marriage, and who had tried to convince them of the beauty of married life as a true and unique expression of mutual commitment of love and responsibility. It had ended with mutual accusations of radicalism, and for months they had all avoided meeting. Then, when their friend's third daughter was born, Nigel and Judith had visited them, and as happens in true friendships, the reasons for their arguments were forgotten.

Marriage or no marriage, however, Nigel and Judith were known among mutual friends as a close-knit match, in which it was impossible to imagine one without the other. Even though they may have lived on two different branches, they were on the same tree.

"I'll be late tonight; I have to study some of the information Margaret has collected for this report. Let's go and have a pizza. What do you say? Do you want to do that?"

"Yes, at Papanino's! We haven't been there for a while."

"Okay, I'll see you at eight thirty."

"Later then."

After the phone call with Judith, Nigel began leafing through Margaret's file. On the cover was the date: November 6.

Knowing his colleague, this was where the research and information gathering had begun. It was almost a month before the storm that had broken out over the lack of garbage disposal which flooded the streets of the city. Nigel had always had to admit, through gritted teeth, that Margaret Hamilton had a nose for news, but even so, to anticipate this, she must have had some tip-off, perhaps from some high-ranking friend of hers.

Nigel had never understood how an uptown girl like Margaret could work at a popular radio station like his. Probably she had been engaged precisely to cover up her upper-class origins and show the world how autonomous she was and how independent from her family's assets, which were notoriously far from small. Nigel had only the editorial meetings in common with her. She was efficient enough for his 'light' transmissions, and he distrusted the reports which were 'committed' to her. "It's easy to be busy when you go to billionaires' parties," was Nigel's terse comment to anyone who asked him for an opinion on Margaret.

The file contained newspaper articles about the Good Environment Centre, one of London's waste disposal companies, perhaps the most important, and about its boss, whom he should have contacted for the interview and who, from the photos, looked like a handsome fifty-year-old. As far as Nigel knew, no scandal had ever made the management of the company look bad.

The story was about the non-collection of rubbish which was throwing local government into disarray, but it wasn't clear to Nigel why he should look into the Good Environment Centre which only dealt with rubbish after collection. Wouldn't it have been more logical to interview some administrator in charge of the matter or even the mayor? Garbage in London was sent for incineration or landfill. Paradoxically, Nigel Tornton, who had never been interested in it before, had learned about it just a year ago, from a report by the Italian news agency Adnkronos on waste disposal systems in large European cities. With regard to the British capital, the piece had not reported any particular critical issues. On the contrary, it underlined the objective of developing differentiated waste collection as a key factor in reducing the amount of rubbish. The discomfort of the last few days and the accumulation of garbage bags seemed to Nigel to be an exceptional matter, and certainly due to contingent factors, first of all, a recent strike by garbage collectors. The uptown girl had obviously blundered, Nigel decided, and she had focused on something that didn't make any sense.

"Or she simply has a broader vision that is escaping you," Judith replied later, in front of a pizza with an intoxicating aroma that only tomato, basil and mozzarella can have.

At Papanino's, the pizza was made with the raw materials in the Italian tradition. The rustic and warm atmosphere of the place had made them feel at home since their first dinner together and, they were sure, had facilitated the happy conclusion of their first appointment outside the hospital. For this reason and for the Italian cuisine they adored, and of which Nino, the owner, was recognised as a master, it had become their favourite restaurant.

"We need to have a broader view," Nigel reiterated after a glass of excellent wine which, he said, went better with pizza than beer. "Lack of trash collection means one thing, and one thing only. That is that the municipal administration has been deficient in recent days, despite all the systems which have applied for years in London. What, we need to ask ourselves, is lacking? So you ask the politician, the mayor or the commissioner on duty for this. The question is for them, not for a waste disposal centre. Citizens pay taxes to keep their streets litter-free. And that's what they must have an answer to.

"Furthermore, it was an inconvenience that lasted several days, and it is because of this that attention should be focused on political and administrative responsibilities. I really think that Margaret's research into waste disposal, and not just collection, has nothing to do with the subject matter of the report."

Judith listened silently, looking at him with her deep black eyes, framed by a perfect oval face and long, silky black hair. She knew well that if, at that moment, she added a single word of reply, he wouldn't have listened to her, too busy with his convictions. She had to wait, let the speech settle, and possibly resume it later. And knowing her man well, she intentionally changed the subject: "Nino's pizza is the best ever."

"Yeah, the best," Nigel said, smiling and taking another bite of his pizza.

Agbogbloshie, November 23

The two Kwabla siblings left the house holding hands. Abenà watched them go towards Father Angelo's Centre. Every morning, she had the impression that they grew bigger and bigger. Kofi for his eight years was very tall, and his slender physique was supported on two long legs, strengthened in recent months, thanks to playing football with the team organised by the missionaries.

The boy had shown great aptitude for the sport and had become their team's best striker. In his personal pantheon, together with the champions of Bayern Munich, whose shirt he wore, were those Ghanaian boys of whose deeds he had heard. Only a little older than him, in 1991 in Italy, Father Angelo's country, they had won the Under 17 World Championships.

Yes, football was important to Kofi, but that was certainly not all. The dark eyes that illuminated his thin and elongated, often melancholic face, told of an already outlined personality: with intelligence but also wisdom, curiosity but also prudence, spirit of initiative but also composure.

Perhaps, it was precisely because of these characteristics that the other children considered him a leader. Kofi did not boast of this tacit recognition, but rather he poured into it an innate propensity to take care of those who, for one reason or another, felt more fragile and weaker. This attention was particularly evident with his little sisters, especially with Ama, closer in age to him and already inextricably linked to him. While Samia at four years old was still attached to her mother, Ama was almost seven and was already crossing the threshold of her independence.

Kofi had begun to attend the school at Father Angelo's Centre. It was run by two nuns who guaranteed didactic continuity in the succession of young teachers who stayed there for a short time, before finding their place elsewhere in the Ghanaian school system recognised among the best in Africa. Ama lived her days mostly away from home, together with her classmates and with Kofi and his friends, when they allowed it.

For almost half a year, since these late-night revels had begun, there was no resistance to this. Small, frail and with an ever-joyful face and vivid curiosity, Ama was now a constant presence in Kofi's party. She was proud of being the only girl allowed in her older brother's group of friends and boasted about it to her classmates.

As the children walked away, Abenà looked at them with pride, forcing herself to imagine for them the most beautiful things they could have in life. When Kofi was born, she had been little more than a child herself, and motherhood had been, as for many Africans, the way to cross the border between playtime and the world of adults. She had accepted it as the natural outcome of a life without alternatives, and she had learned to really love the husband who had chosen her.

She had serenely accepted his decision to seek better conditions in the capital. Among the women of the north, he had preserved the pride of bearing and the elegance of the movement. He rarely smiled, except at the children, but had never said a word or shown a feeling of disobedience or frustration, never had his voice lost its calmness or the firmness of its reassuring timbre, never had his eyes shown hatred or anger, never a tear, whether in joy or pain, not even in the difficulties of migration and in those of the conditions in which his family had found themselves: full of love but besieged by the hell of Agbogbloshie.

Here, Ama and Samia had come into the world, before Abenà's body was unable to give them further siblings. Her face and body, despite the signs of more the efforts than of the time, remained beautiful, reminding her of her husband's ever-present passion and also of the glances that sometimes met her outside the house. Her features were ready to soften whenever her gaze fell on the three little creatures. She continued to watch them walk to their gate and silently called out to God and the ancestors to bless their lives.

"Kofi, why do only some of us have to go to the sorceress? Francis and his sister, for example, don't have to," Ama asked her brother.

"Probably because we are privileged."

"Privileged? But we have to wake up every morning when everyone continues to sleep and then walk in the dark to go to the sorceress. Let her do all the things that... that... I still don't understand what they're for! When we get home, the others still eat and drink their milk, after having stayed up until late. What privilege is that?"

For her age, Ama had already shown great argumentative and critical skills. Her brother had learned to take these observations into account.

"I don't know, Ama, but do you remember that Father Angelo said that if we do this it is good for us and also for other children?"

"Perhaps, Kofi, but I don't understand why all this is good. All I know is that I'm very tired of getting up early."

The children arrived at the Centre, in front of which the

silhouette of a tall, robust man stood out among those of six children in a circle around him. They were waiting, as they often did, since it wasn't unusual for Kofi and Ama to be the last ones to arrive. The man, Father Angelo, welcomed them with a smile. He was not yet fifty years old, but what was striking, in addition to the intense blue eyes in a reassuring face, was the thick hair, already white. That hair and fair complexion stood out even more in contrast with the dark shirt that he always wore, even if without other signs of religious affiliation.

"Good morning, Father Angelo!"

"Good morning, children! So, we're all here now and we're all ready. Ready?" he said forcefully, perhaps to give another wake-up call to the children who still seemed to be dozing on their feet.

The party walked up a dirt road towards the new complex of houses on the edge of the neighbourhood, away from the landfill. The children walked in single file holding hands. Father Angelo closed the strange little procession.

"Father Angelo, is it true that the sorceress will go away in a few days?" Kofi asked.

"Yes, children, she will leave us at the end of this month."

"Really?" asked one of the older children in the party, whose father had wanted to name him Martin after hearing the story of Martin Luther King. "He too, with this name, will do great things in life," he had said, with conviction.

"But why?" Ama asked. It was she who always asked this question, one the most difficult to answer, to the point that her nickname in the group was 'Miss Why'.

"She has to go and meet other children who live in other places," replied the religious man.

"But are they faraway places?" Kwame asked in a very

feeble voice. He was a boy of the same age as Ama, short in stature and with quite a paunch. Compared to the others, his legs and arms were also fleshier, and his little face had two beautiful round cheeks which, when he laughed, filled his face.

"Yes, I also wanted to ask the same question as Palletta," said Ama, calling her companion by the nickname given to him by his physical appearance.

"Yes, she will go far away, children."

"But will we see her again?" Kwame asked again.

"No, I do not think so. Or at least we won't see her again for a long time."

The silence of the children and their sorry faces surprised the priest, who hadn't expected it. He would have thought that they would be glad they didn't have to get up so early anymore. But children are unpredictable and he, who knew them well, sometimes forgot the lessons that they can teach adults at any time.

"But if we never see her again, we have to give her a present! Mother always says that gifts must be given to those who come and to those who go away." The strong, ringing voice of Nelson, an eight-year-old boy, broke the mournful silence. His eyes suddenly widened at the news of the sorceress' departure, as if he was waking up just then, in a mixture of surprise, displeasure and, at the same time, excitement, at the thought of the gift.

"And what present could we give her?" Nii asked. He was the nephew of one of the elders of the community who gravitated around Father Angelo's Centre. Respected by all he was a jealous guardian of the traditions of the Ahafo, the people of his homeland in the north, and those of the Kwabla family, the stories of which he never got tired of telling. He had the same narrow nose and well-defined cut of the mouth of his grandfather Nii, and at the age of seven, he too loved to try his hand at telling stories. Above all, he loved the story of when he had been with his father in Accra, a place the other children had never seen, where, according to him, there were houses as high as the sky, the streets were of a very hard black earth that didn't budge when you walked on it, and were filled with large painted signs, taller and wider than the front of his house. But the other children tended not to believe him, even though such things sometimes appeared on the television set in Father Angelo's Centre. They watched the championship football matches there, often those of the Naples team, the legendary team that the priest always spoke of, via the video tapes that arrived regularly from Italy.

"Let's make her a necklace of beads and candy," Ama said with a determined air.

"*Buaaaaa*... and what will she do with it? She's a sorceress! She doesn't need these sissy things!" Kwame silenced her, maintaining his conflicting and fluctuating relationship with the same aged Ama. These quarrels were punctuated by "You are no longer my friend, Palletta di grease," and, "I don't want to see you anymore, sissy that you are," alternated with great displays of affection, hugs and kisses, with corollary phrases such as, "You will be my friend for life, Kwame," and, "Not a day goes by without us playing together, Ama."

Father Angelo smiled as he listened to the excitement of the boys and their involvement in the choice of the gift, a decision that he knew well should be theirs alone, so he should avoid giving suggestions.

"I found this! In my uncle's warehouse I have a laptop that I found in the junkyard and I'm fixing it. We could give you that, if we fix it right!" Nelson exclaimed.

"But do you think we'll be able to make it work?" asked

Aziz, a frail-looking seven-year-old boy who in recent weeks, due to increasingly frequent illness, left the house almost only for his morning appointments with the sorceress. His house was similar to that of the Kwabla's nearby but appeared to be in much poorer condition.

Eight of his family lived in the single room that served as a kitchen and bedroom: Aziz, his five much older brothers, his mother and grandfather. The father rarely returned home. Once he had heard his mother say to a foreign lady who worked for the same 'humanitarian association' as the music man, that she wished her husband would never come back because in addition to making her pregnant again, he would have transmitted further disease. Aziz did not know what his mum was suffering from, or what ailments his dad had passed on to her, but in his heart, he would have instead wanted to see him and play with him. His brothers were already going to work in the centre of Accra, sometimes returning in the evening, and at other times, absent for days. Aziz didn't know what they did, but thanks to them, Mum was able to buy food for the whole family.

"Of course, yes! By now I've learned to fix old computers, radios and stereos that I get from the junkyard. Trust me," Nelson said.

"But if you keep all these and don't give them to recuperators, you'll earn less," Kofi objected.

"Yes, maybe, but I enjoy fixing old equipment… it's the only toy I have." Nelson added in a lower voice, "And then one day I'll need it for my work, when I'm older."

"Okay, you convinced me." Kofi's confident voice sounded like a sentence. "Let's go to your uncle's warehouse, all right? Let's start working on it."

"Very well!", "Yes, how beautiful!", "Perfect!": each of the children expressed their approval.

"I'm here too!" Osagyefo said vehemently, with all the voice in his body.

He was the youngest of the group, the one who always followed everyone without ever complaining. He rarely got angry, mainly when the older ones didn't let him play football. As good and fast as he was, in fact, he was too small and thin to emerge unscathed from matches in which, despite the watchful eye of Father Angelo, there was no shortage of clashes that were foul.

"Ah, but you are awake, Osagyefo!" the priest exclaimed, smiling at the boy. "Guys, I'm sure the sorceress will be very happy with the gift you want to give her."

The small party had now arrived in front of a house far from the landfill, in an area of new construction along the road to Accra. In other places it would have passed unnoticed, but this was a striking structure, a wooden building on a stone foundation, with large glass windows and access from a veranda through a sturdy wooden door that closed with keys. Father Angelo shook the chain of the bell attached to the wall decisively: the door was opened by a tall, blonde woman in a long white dress that reached to her calves. She grinned and invited the small group inside. "Good morning, I've been waiting for you," she said.

London, December 5

"Nigel, what's this about?" Margaret asked, stunned by Nigel's call at eight ten, just after his radio broadcast. It was a bit strange that call from someone who had never expressed great sympathy for her, who had never exchanged a word with her beyond the ritual 'Good morning' and 'Good evening'.

"Well, I heard the happy news and I wanted to celebrate with you and find out how the baby is doing," he replied, fully aware of how unbelievable this was.

Margaret pretended to play along for just an instant. "Thank you! I'm fine; the baby is fine. Now can you tell me exactly what you need, given that the happy event happened a week ago and you're the only one on the radio who hasn't called me before?"

Nigel's dislike for the woman he called 'Miss I-know-everything' strengthened, but he understood that it was useless to drag things out. "It's about the garbage piece you started. Since you are rightfully on maternity leave, the boss assigned it to me. It should air on December 11."

There was a brief pause and then the woman commented dryly, "What's that got to do with you, Nigel? It's a serious piece. I never thought the boss would give it to you."

Nigel didn't think anything about this woman could touch him, but this time he felt offended, struck to the core of his professionalism. But it also prompted to wonder how, in all his years on the radio, he could have given such an impression of superficiality.

"What exactly do you want to know, Nigel?"

"I wanted to ask you for some explanations. I wonder why you haven't focused your attention on the politics of municipal councils in recent days. I would have expected – I don't know – an interview with the councillor, for example, or better still with the mayor, while instead, you concentrated on a waste disposal company."

Again, there was silence on the other end of the phone, and Nigel, convinced he had embarrassed his colleague, reiterated the point, "In short, garbage isn't a highly problematic issue in London. We may have been in crisis for a few days due to the garbage collectors' strike, and due to the bad weather, but we both know that it is not one of the critical issues of our city. So, it's fine to do the piece, but I don't understand why approaching it from the point of view of disposal which, from what I know, doesn't work too badly anyway."

Margaret's voice was firm and sure. "Obviously, you didn't understand what my piece is supposed to be about. In any case, I'll give you a hand, only and exclusively for the good conclusion, if possible, of what I've started. Go read Lawrence Summers' statements in 1991 when he was head of the World Bank, and then maybe you'll get there too. And if you get there, chances are people will care. I salute you."

With this she closed the conversation, and Nigel was unable to answer her adequately, strengthening his conviction regarding the arrogance and antipathy of his colleague. But he had to admit that the idea intrigued him. What did Summers have to do with a London rubbish story? Nigel knew very little about Summers. He vaguely remembered that he had been awarded the John Bates Clark Medal for his studies in macroeconomics, and in addition to having been chief economist of the World Bank in the early

1990s, he had also held several senior positions during the Clinton administration. Nigel didn't know anything else, nor was he very interested. He immediately began an internet search to try to understand how, according to Margaret, Lawrence Summers could have some connection with his project.

The first piece of news that emerged was the so-called *Summers memo* of 1991, a memo on trade liberalisation written by Lant Pritchett and signed by Summers himself in his role as chief economist of the World Bank. Nigel had never dealt with concepts such as trade and liberalisation: he knew that Marx had written *Das Kapital* and he remembered something of the high school debates between left and right student groups about the capitalist system and Thatcher's neo-liberalism, but that was all.

Starting to read the *Summers memo*, Nigel remembered those high school debates, and even more, the evenings that his parents had spent with their politically engaged friends. In both cases, there would have been bottles of whisky, ashtrays full of butts and clouds of smoke above the heated discussions. They were very different times.

The text of the memo, as reported by Wikipedia, read:

DATE: December 12, 1991
TO: Distribution
FR: Lawrence H. Summers
Subject: GEP

'Dirty' Industries: Just between you and me, shouldn't the World Bank be encouraging MORE migration of the dirty industries to the LDCs [Least Developed Countries]? I can think of three reasons:

1) The measurements of the costs of health impairing pollution depends on the foregone earnings from increased morbidity and mortality. From this point of view a given amount of health impairing pollution should be done in the country with the lowest cost, which will be the country with the lowest wages. I think the economic logic behind dumping a load of toxic waste in the lowest wage country is impeccable and we should face up to that.

2) The costs of pollution are likely to be non-linear as the initial increments of pollution probably have very low cost. I've always thought that under-populated countries in Africa are vastly UNDER-polluted, their air quality is probably vastly inefficiently low compared to Los Angeles or Mexico City. Only the lamentable facts that so much pollution is generated by non-tradable industries (transport, electrical generation) and that the unit transport costs of solid waste are so high prevent world welfare enhancing trade in air pollution and waste.

3) The demand for a clean environment for aesthetic and health reasons is likely to have very high income elasticity. The concern over an agent that causes a one in a million change in the odds of prostrate[sic] cancer is obviously going to be much higher in a country where people survive to get prostrate[sic] cancer than in a country where under 5 mortality is 200 per thousand. Also, much of the concern over industrial atmosphere discharge is about visibility impairing particulates. These discharges may have very little direct health impact. Clearly trade in goods that embody aesthetic pollution concerns could be welfare enhancing. While production is mobile the consumption of pretty air is a non-tradable.

The problem with the arguments against all of these proposals for more pollution in LDCs (intrinsic rights to certain goods, moral reasons, social concerns, lack of adequate markets, etc.) could be turned around and used more or less effectively against every Bank proposal for liberalization. Signed: Lawrence Summers.

    Nigel reread the text three times: the first time to understand its logic, which was aberrant according to his sensitivity; the second, weighing up every single word, to realise the general, and not merely economic, value it could have; and the third to marvel at how such a text could come out of the World Bank.

    It was incredible that it was so easy to read it – on sites available to everyone. One name, one click, and anyone had the opportunity to see this memo. Nigel continued his search, leafing through article titles and various comments, until he came across a piece of news reported in Harvard Magazine in an article Toxic Memo on May 10, 2001, in which Pritchett had declared that the *Summers memo* had been manipulated and retouched, and was "a deliberate fraud and forgery aimed at discrediting Larry and the World Bank," and suggesting that the tenor and purpose of the memo was to be only 'sarcastic', to solicit international reflection.

    Somehow, Nigel was heartened by these declarations, almost as if they had made him change his mind about the arrogance of power, perhaps not so shameless to the point of planning and formalising how to destroy one part of the world for the benefit of another hemisphere. But the research gave him much more. The presumed logic of polluting where it is more convenient to dispose of waste, where work costs less, and where it is easier to compensate for the damage caused by contamination seemed to translate into implications far beyond the mere 'cheaper'. The more he read articles published on sites he scrolled through in sequence on his computer screen, the more he felt he had to go deeper to discover a reality that was unimaginable for him.

Agbogbloshie. How do you live in Africa's largest e-waste dump, where computers go to die as our e-waste dumps poison Africa? Outrageous! Africa is being used as a dumping ground for hazardous waste and electronics. Whether the memorandum was true or playful, it seemed to be the theorisation of a tragic reality, denounced on the internet.

Agbogbloshie, November 23

Aurora, dawn twilight and sunset twilight are features of temperate countries. Accra is almost at the Equator. At those latitudes, day and night take turns quickly.

In the evening, the sun plunges rapidly into the Atlantic. In the Port of Tema, the lights of dozens and dozens of container ships shine. Their shipments, mainly used technological materials, will soon swell the market that winds along the road towards the city, a market for increasingly rundown objects, on up to the Agbogbloshie landfill.

For a short time, the eternal black smoke that hangs over that heap of electronic garbage, is tinged blood red. It doesn't last long, just long enough to highlight the shadows of bodies which, from afar, look like shapeless beings without identity. This is the time when the elderly, young people and children, who wander around it during the day, leave the site, bending down to pick up the pieces, and then either throw them back on the ground or place them in their baskets before looking for more.

The children are the first to line up to deliver their loot to the salvagers and then hurry home – those who have homes – for dinner. Kofi walked slowly beside his little sister, feeling the tiredness of the day but also the joy of the thought of the fufu with chicken and peanuts that his mother had promised him. The idea of his favourite dish relieved him of the drudgery and ankylosis of hours searching for computer hard drives, modems and wires. He marvelled at how his sister, on the other hand, was always cheerful and never lost the desire to sing some invented word to the tunes she already knew. For days now it had been the song that was supposed to accompany her marriage to the Prince of England. It was Father Angelo who had told her about the young man in an officer's uniform who was photographed in an old magazine found in the dump, packaging between two computers in a container.

"When I grow up, I will go to England, and I will have joy and love with the prince..." she sang, occasionally hinting at a few dance steps. "Kofi, do you think I should know better English to marry the prince?"

"Well, yes. Definitely yes. You should ask school for a few more lessons or have them teach you some of the songs Nelson listens to."

"The ones recorded on the tape you found in the field? I had thought about it too. I'll ask him tonight. The day I meet the prince, I'll have to understand him when he asks me to marry him. Because if I don't understand him, how can I say yes?

"When I grow up, and I meet the prince, when he asks me I will say..."

Ama resumed dancing, while her brother looked at her, not knowing whether to try to believe with her or to break that dream.

By now they were close to the recuperators who were already weighing the material delivered by other children. Between them the two little siblings recognised Nelson and Martin, lined up with their baskets.

"Hi, guys, we didn't see you in the field. When did you arrive?" Kofi asked them.

"We've been here all afternoon, but we went to work in the part where the adults go... there's better stuff there," replied Nelson, adding: "So tomorrow, everyone will come to me to prepare a gift for the sorceress. In my uncle's warehouse, there is everything we need, and there is also a nice battery-operated tape recorder. I have many batteries, still good, so we can also hear the songs from the tape I found. I'm memorising them."

"*Shhhh!*" Kofi hushed him quickly, continuing in a low voice, "you know you mustn't be heard talking about the white sorceress by the recuperators! Do you remember what happened to Jeffrey? The recuperators stopped buying anything from him as soon as they learned that he was visiting the white sorceress. Even our parents told us not to tell anyone about it."

"And Jeffrey had to stop coming with us to the sorceress so he could get back to work," Ama recalled, pointing her index finger at Nelson.

"I know. You're right."

"Kofi, are you sure what the white sorceress does is good for us? Why do we have to go when the other kids don't?" asked Martin.

Before Kofi could answer, the shouts of a recuperator drowned out their voices: "Come on, hurry up kids! Do you want to show me how much you have collected or do you want to stay and chat?"

Kofi and Ama handed over their loot to the man whom they called 'Mountain', due to his exceptional stature, and waited for the check.

"Hey, you'll be hitting five kilos each soon. And for today here's already four thousand cedis for you, little boy, and for your sister, two thousand," said Montagna.

"In the meantime, what do you think? I'll marry the Prince of England as soon as I grow up and he'll come and buy everything you have!" Ama said to him, raising her little face and frowning with a look of defiance.

Kofi looked sternly at his sister to silence her, while Nelson and Aziz stiffened, fearful of a terrible reaction from Montagna. The man looked at the little girl without understanding whether to be offended or not.

"Run away, little girl; that's best for you," he concluded.

It was then Nelson and Martin's turn.

"You, on the other hand, are still scarce. You'd better put in a little more effort. Here are two thousand cedis a head."

"Come to me tomorrow to work on the gift for the sorceress," Nelson said again, as soon as they resumed their journey home, away from Montagna. "The computer I recovered is still in good shape. I wanted to fix it for me, but I'll find another one."

"But the tools to fix it, screws, cables; do we have everything?" Kofi asked.

"Woh! In my uncle's warehouse you can find all the tools you want! I fixed the tape recorder and once I fixed a small radio. No problem."

"We have to start today. We have only a few days before the sorceress leaves. Today I found one of those things that drive the computer to write... what's it called... mouse?"

"Yes, Kofi, mouse. Great! But we can't do it today, because it's my mum's birthday. But trust us, we can do it! I had already started working on the computer: it's a laptop and it's still in good condition. We could get a nice amount if we resell it."

"Nelson, that's for the sorceress. Don't get any other ideas!" Ama said.

"I know, Ama. I know."

"Nelson, can we use the cassette player you got from your uncle too?" added the little girl.

"What do you need it for?"

"I'd like to hear your tape of English music, the one you like so much."

"You mean the one with songs by that singer named David Bowie?"

"I don't know the singer's name... it's the songs that you sing."

"Okay, but what do you need it for? Don't tell me you like them too?"

"No, but I have to learn English very well, so when I'm married to the Prince of England, I'll have no trouble understanding what he's saying."

With the exception of Kofi, the other children burst into laughter.

"Do you really believe this story? You, married to the Prince of England! But you will never meet him in your life!" Nelson yelled at her.

Ama glared at him, hurt. Her eyes began to water and her lips to tighten. She tried to hold back the tears by squeezing her hands between the folds of the skirt of her dress. In that moment Nelson and Martin realised how foolish and cruel they had been to their little friend, to the girl in their group. They wanted to apologise, and reassure her that instead she would meet her prince and live in his castle in beautiful clothes.

"I'm sure they didn't mean to offend you, Ama," Kofi said, looking sternly at his friends, "and I'm sure Nelson will not only play you the music, but he'll teach you his favourite song."

"Yes, Ama, I will teach you *Life on Mars*. It's a slow song you can dance to while hugging your prince," was all Nelson managed.

Kofi tried to take Ama's hand to walk back to the house, but her small hands were still wrapped in her dress, and her gaze fixed on Nelson. Slowly, however, her face began to relax and the lines in that minute oval faded. Ama's eyes were moist from the crying she had blocked out of pride. She, the only female in that group of all male friends, would not now pass for the weakest.

"How does *Life on Mars* go? Can you sing it to me?" she asked Nelson in a soothing tone.

The boy smiled and began to sing it as the group headed home.

"Do you like that, Ama?" Kofi asked, finally managing to hold her hand.

"Very much."

"Can you tell me exactly what the words mean? I don't understand them," Martin asked. In his family, the language spoken was tribal and he had learned English on the street, only just beginning to study it in school.

"Certainly. I don't remember it all, but the first words go like this:

> "*It's a god-awful small affair*
> *To the girl with the mousy hair*
> *But her mummy is yelling, "No!"*
> *And her daddy has told her to go*
> *But her friend is nowhere to be seen*
> *Now she walks through her sunken dream*
> *To the seat with the clearest view*
> *And she's hooked to the silver screen*
> *But the film is a saddening bore*
> *For she's lived it ten times or more*
> *She could spit in the eyes of fools*
> *As they ask her to focus on...*"

"But what is the meaning of these words? I don't understand!"

Martin repeated.

"I really don't know... but I like the song. I too would like to write songs like this."

"Why? Have you ever made-up songs?"

"No, Martin, not really yet, but... What's wrong with you?" He looked at Ama. "Why are you crying now? I told you that I will teach you this song, that you can also dance with the Prince of England."

The little girl's face was now completely wet with tears. Kofi squeezed her hand tighter and leaned over to wipe it away. "Don't cry Ama, you will dance with your prince. I promise you," he repeated too.

But now Ama couldn't have said why she was crying. She only felt a great emptiness that she had never felt before listening to the words of the song. She wasn't the only one to have dreams; a grey-haired girl dreamed too, but she was left alone and her friend hadn't shown up either. Ama remained silent and unable to stop the tears. She wanted to explain, but she couldn't. She didn't know the words to say how she was feeling and that scared her.

She still needed her prince; she still needed to believe that one day she would meet him and spend her whole life with him, pampered and spoiled, with delicious sweets, and long and precious dresses like the ones she'd seen in the magazine she'd found in the dump. It didn't matter if it was just a dream; it was better than reality for her. She took her hand away from that of her brother, who was still in front of her, to wipe away her tears, and started walking on her own.

The others watched as Kofi followed her, stepping back. They did the same, as if they were a procession of little knights following their princess. They greeted each other with barely a nod as they reached their homes.

From the open doors they could see the women preparing dinner and the little ones playing on the ground, while the men talked on the street. It was the time when everyone left the day's labours and families reunited. The smells of the food overcame the constant bad smell that the wind carried from the landfill. For the children, everything represented safety, of family, of home.

But that day, a veil of sadness had settled over Nelson, Martin, Kofi, and above all Ama. Something had changed: it didn't take much, a joke, a song, to make it clear to all of them that that road from the landfill to their homes was the only reality they had; that their every desire travelled far, too far.

London, December 5

Nigel stopped for a coffee break, his daily drug. As he used to say, he could kill for a cup of coffee, and contrary to the trend of pods and machines advertised by famous actors, he preferred mocha. The important thing was the 'ritual' of coffee and being able to stop whatever he was doing to follow the small steps necessary to enjoy his dark hot elixir: pour the water into the mocha pot, dose the black powder which never flattened with the teaspoon, close the machine and put it on the fire.

"Do you want to put all this – the wait for the rumbling of the coffee, the smell of its warm aroma – with the mechanical inserting of a cold capsule into a metal and plastic machine?" he kept repeating to Judith, who had already opted for the convenience and speed of those small pods in various colours, according to their multiple blends.

Nigel needed his break right now, and as he waited for his warm drink to brew, he lit a cigarette. It was a typical binomial, coffee and a cigarette, which helped him to catch his breath and rework his thoughts and collect his sensations.

Despite his criticisms of his parents' generation, he had never been particularly sensitive to hot social and political issues, or those which for many of his friends also meant sit-ins, demonstrations and discussions. His music was enough for him, and it was his home in which to take refuge with Judith, his friends, and to drink with them.

This was his life and he liked it the way it was. After all, he earned enough to indulge in every whim he might have, considering that his vices were modest. He had never had a particular fondness for cars or motorcycles; the sixty-square-metre apartment in Regent Street, given to him by his parents, was more than sufficient, and he had the means to treat himself to some nice trips from time to time, away from the traditional tourist destinations and always to interesting places.

In short, he was fine, and paid little attention to politically correct issues, such as social rights or the environment. Perhaps it was because he had no children, as his friends suggested in their vain attempts to educate him on the path of social commitment.

Perhaps. But Nigel found it equally false to suggest that you have to look after the world only for the interests of your children: either you are unconditionally interested in the health of the world and the lives of others or your interest is utilitarian and selfish. He was very categorical about this.

The aroma of coffee had already filled the small kitchenette, not far from the desks of journalists and collaborators. It was pleasant and the most frequented room at the newspaper, a place where you could take a break and, if necessary, have a chat with colleagues. The window allowed smokers to exit directly from the kitchen onto the terrace. But Nigel wasn't the only one who lit a cigarette in the kitchen and forgot to go outside to smoke it.

The smell of coffee always attracted other people, and so it was that day.

"Hi, Nigel, you made the coffee, huh?" was Robert Bradley's rhetorical question, peeking in the door.

"If you want, I'll give you a drop, but after that I'll be thoroughly satisfied."

"Always generous," replied his colleague, also lighting a

cigarette.

"Robert, have you ever worked on landfill projects – other than in your own home?" Between the two, jokes, even dark ones, were usual.

"There are no incinerators sufficient for my house. Seriously, I have sometimes dealt with some of them in news pieces, nothing in-depth though. But what interests you in particular?"

"I'm running a feature on landfills that Miss Sympathy started," Bradley and Nigel shared similar views on Margaret Hamilton, "and I came across the landfills of Africa, which are largely replenished with our rubbish."

"Yes, I know our dear friend was dealing with rubbish, but if I remember correctly, it was about the accumulation of garbage due to the strike by the garbage men."

"Indeed, it seemed so, but then it took a different line that I'm also interested in."

"You interested in Margaret's idea? Oh my! Give me a coffee right away so I can take this in!" Bradley continued seriously: "If this the way you're going with this topic, I know what it is about because, by chance, I found myself talking about it some time ago with two friends of Micaela's who are writing a report for a non-profit organisation committed precisely to this. They seemed very well prepared. I knew nothing about it, and I was really struck by their stories of cities built on rubbish and the economic traffic that surrounds them."

"I started reading something on the internet, and I will continue to read more," Nigel answered, "but I would very much like to talk about it live with someone who has direct knowledge. Do you think I could meet them? Can you put me in touch with them?"

"Sure, they're friends of Micaela's. I'll ask for their number.

So, why did you really get into this piece?"

"I don't really know. Perhaps because it will be the first which does not talk about music, and I want to give it my best shot."

"I'll call Micaela and put you in touch with them."

"Okay, thank you. By the way, how is Micaela?"

"As usual: fervent Amnesty activist, bad cook, but an excellent lover."

"Well... what can I say? Why don't you marry her?"

"After you, my dear Nigel. After you."

The day passed quickly, and in the late afternoon, Nigel was still in front of the computer, scrolling through articles about Africa, landfills, trade and waste. He printed out the news that seemed most interesting and wrote down names and dates. The folder of material was getting bigger and bigger. Everything was close at hand, but it all remained distant from his life and his mind. Yes, he was beginning to know the facts, but he knew that he lacked both a global vision and the empathy necessary to bind them together for his piece. He knew that the success of his broadcasts was just that: getting to the heart of the issues, making them live in his skin, thus transferring to his listeners the same passion that had enraptured and involved him. It came easy and naturally to him, with music becoming a part of his DNA. But not with news found only on the internet.

This is precisely the problem of information today, he began to think, everyone knows everything very easily. Yet few are really aware of what is happening around us. We settle for approximate news and never go into it to really understand it. We think we live in a world that is a glass bell, but in the end, we know nothing of what is happening before our eyes. A small click on the internet is enough for us, and we convince ourselves that we know the universe up close, without needing to bother about it too much. From London to Dubai, from Dubai to Rome, from Rome to Moscow and so on: a distance of hundreds of thousands of kilometres evaporated with a simple click.

His mobile buzzed, rousing him.

"Tell me I'm your friend. Tomorrow at twelve I've made an appointment for you with Micaela's two friends, Joel Jansken and Kurt Oliver, at the Café Noir, round the corner from here."

"You are my friend."

Agbogbloshie, November 24

For the children of Agbogbloshie, the best nights were when the Baba told them a story. He was the oldest man who lived there, the wisest, and the most authoritative. In reality, no one knew how old he really was, but his very thin white hair, his beard that was once thick but now sparse, his wrinkled and flaccid skin and his muscles no longer supple, spoke for themselves. His eyes had the opaque transparency of someone who no longer sees. He never smiled, as if he had forgotten the way or could find no reason to. But those lightless eyes and that unsmiling face were good. No one had ever seen him kneeling on the *sajjÿda*, the Islamic prayer rug, and he certainly wasn't a priest like Father Angelo. But everyone there, the few Christians and the many Muslims, considered him the closest being to God, the one able to listen to God best and fully understand his message. Everyone knew that old Baba knew how to recognise God's will, and what was right for people to do. And Father Angelo, who spent a lot of time with the Baba, was quite convinced of it too.

No one knew whether the Baba was born in those parts or not. Someone said that he had come as a young man from a different and distant land. However, he had arrived alone and remained alone. He had never had a family, and this suggested to many that he had never taken a wife, precisely to devote himself to those in need of him, a bit like Father Angelo. Certainly, he had no family members to look after him in his old age. But among those people who had nothing that was superfluous and yet were ready to share what was necessary, it was a point of honour that they lacked for nothing.

For the neighbours, it was normal to bring the Baba some of the food they cooked for their families every day and tidy up his house when necessary. There were always young men vying for the honour of filling his water tank or supporting him as he moved about in that chaotic place. And many adults, including Father Angelo, often stopped to greet him, each time leaving a little beer or a little tobacco. Those men, those who had never mixed with those in any gigantic city and who seemed to have lost all sense of right and wrong, saw in the Baba a legacy of a more decent life than they had experienced in their old tribal villages.

It was not uncommon for his people to ask him to settle a dispute about ownership of something, an unpaid debt or an offence. Of course, the Baba's opinions were not binding, but it seemed to everyone to be more useful to turn to him rather than to any judge or any authority. Someone said, as an established truth, that he had been a great hunter and that as a young man he had killed a lion with his bare hands and absorbed its strength, and perhaps some magical power.

"Ah yes, Hercules with the Nemean lion," Father Angelo said to himself when he heard those stories. But then he remembered that even in the Bible, the Word of God, it is said that Samson killed a lion with his bare hands, with a prodigal strength given to him by God. And he promised himself to be more cautious and less sarcastic.

But to the children, Baba was only Grandfather Baba, a grandfather more grandfather than the others, who told fantastic stories of exceptional children and wild animals of the forest, all with morals he never failed to explain. Whenever he showed his intention of telling a tale, the news spread in a flash, and dozens of children crowded in front of his chair, outside his house.

However, for the older youth, now too far from their fairy tale years and too self-confident to ask for advice, old Baba was nothing more than a component of a time that wasn't theirs, a time without music, beers, cigarettes and those places near the port that attracted them and where people much tougher than them enlisted labour.

That evening, the Baba chose an ancient fairy tale from Kenya, one of the places where he was said to have lived. Virtually everyone knew it, including the many adults who had also stopped by with their children. But there was the man's warm and deep voice, the hypnotic calm of his articulated words, to convey a quiet sweetness to those who listened to him.

"In a savannah on the edge of a great forest and an even greater desert, lived a beautiful giraffe: she was agile and slender, taller than any other. She was much admired by all the animals, and because of this, she also became very proud. This meant that she no longer had respect for anyone. She didn't help anyone who turned to her. Her only passion was to go around all day to show off her beauty, saying to one and the other: 'Look at me, I am the most beautiful.' The animals, fed up with her boasting, teased her, but the giraffe was too vain to care for them.

"One day the monkey decided to teach her a lesson. So he decided to flatter her with words that caressed the giraffe's ears: 'How beautiful you are! How tall you are! Your height is not reached by any other animal.' And he led her to the tallest palm tree in a nearby oasis. There the monkey asked the giraffe to get the dates that stood high and were the sweetest. Her neck was very long, but no matter how hard she tried to stretch it even more, she couldn't reach the fruit. Then the monkey, with a leap, jumped on her back, climbed along her neck and hoisted himself on top of the giraffe's head, managing to grab the desired fruits.

"Once back on the ground, the monkey said to the giraffe: 'You see, my dear, you are the tallest, the most beautiful, but you cannot live without others.' The giraffe learned the lesson and from that day on she was much more cooperative and friendly with the other animals."

At the end of the story, the Baba stopped for a few seconds and then resumed, "Children, it often happens that, for one reason or another, we think we don't need others and that our life can go on while we ignore those around us. But each of us, even if the most beautiful and intelligent, is nobody if he can't count on the affection and friendship of his neighbours. I ask you to always remember this in your life: without the help and collaboration of those around us, we can do nothing."

"And the stars? It was you who told us that each of us has a star that is our friend and guides us," ventured a little boy.

"It is true. And I'm glad you listened well. Remember that each of us has a star in the sky that protects us and brings our wishes to God's ears. God loves us and knows what is best for us. He listens to what we ask and reads our hearts. But also remember the story of the giraffe, and that our wishes can come true with the help of our companions and friends. Life has meaning only if we share it with them." Then Baba seemed to address the adults: "Solitary joys don't last long."

London, December 6

"Why are you interested in this investigation?" asked Kurt.

Kurt was a large, tall man with a long, dark oval face, marked by an important nose between elongated and deep black eyes. In line with his name, he evoked a Saxon origin, but the physiognomy of his face also betrayed oriental roots. It was he, by age and by approach, who assumed responsibilities and made the decisions in his field of work. His colleague, Joel, younger in years, seemed instead to have an aptitude more for reflection than for decision-making. He was equally tall, with undoubtedly Nordic colours and clear and lively eyes. Joel had very gentle manners, sometimes perhaps he seemed insecure, typical of one who is fresh from studies, theories and his first job. These were the two leads Robert had found for Nigel.

"Let me introduce myself first," said Nigel, inviting them to a table in the Café Noir.

"You're right. Sorry for my abruptness. Sometimes I don't even realise it anymore."

"No problem," replied Nigel who, all in all, didn't dislike Kurt's manners: they showed a certain frankness of behaviour and probably the will not to get lost in useless conversations. Nigel was the same in his work. "Can we order something too?" he added, pointing to a young waitress who had approached.

"Coffee for me, thanks," Kurt said.

"And for you, Joel?"

"Me too. Thank you, with milk."

"Three coffees, then."

As soon as the girl left, Nigel resumed the conversation. "You probably already know that I'm a radio journalist. Up until two days ago, I only dealt with music, in a program that I host in the morning." The two listened to him without interruption. "Don't ask me why, but the day before yesterday, my boss wanted me to start dealing with something else, with politics and society, and assigned me my first piece – on waste disposal. I thought I would be talking about the rubbish on the streets of our city, but due to a series of circumstances, I found myself directing my research towards the landfills of Africa. And the more I go on, the more what I read intrigues me. I don't know much about it apart from what I could find on the internet, and I would like to understand it better. That's all."

"Okay, clear. But I repeat the question: why do you want to know? Do you really want to take the matter seriously?" Kurt realised from Nigel's surprised and annoyed look that he needed to explain himself better. "We can talk to each other clearly, can't we?"

"Absolutely."

"You see, Nigel, we could spend two hours, and it wouldn't even be enough to begin to talk about what happens in African landfills and why it happens. I would be happy to tell those who don't know about the reality that I have discovered through my work. But I would like to know why. Out of mere curiosity, which may well be better than wasting time playing darts and drinking beer? Or to reinforce a five-minute news report, which many then forget? This too would be fine with me because I would have the hope that someone among the thousands of sleepy people who listen to your show might be intrigued, even a little. Or for what else?'

Nigel was beginning to feel insulted, professionally and personally. Kurt might have made his social activism more than just a job but a reason for his very existence; however, Nigel wasn't willing to submit to accept such an arrogant attitude nor did he understand why Kurt was so unsympathetic.

"Kurt, like I said, I have a story to do, and I'm interested in hearing as much as I can. I didn't stop to make a psychological analysis of the typology of my interest, whether it was limited to the piece or if it is affecting my life to the point of dealing with this issue in future. I guess that is what you mean by 'for what else', right? I don't think the feedback from my humble little report of a few minutes on the radio will be the most popular. I don't think I'll win the Pulitzer Prize for this work. And I don't think it will be of such importance as to change the fate of the world nor do I have some kind of wishful thinking. To be honest, I asked for this meeting just to get some simple explanations from those who know more than me. That's all. But if it's too unimportant for you to stay here with me and talk about it, we can stop now."

After a moment of silence, and with a smile and a more affable voice, Kurt reassured him, "No, no, of course not."

Nigel still didn't understand Kurt's attitude, which seemed to be testing him somehow, but he didn't want to make useless assumptions. He just needed some news. Luckily, at that moment the waitress arrived with a tray containing the three coffees, a jug of milk and a saucer with the bill on it. "It's mine," Nigel said, blocking Kurt who had already reached for his wallet. Kurt let it go.

"What exactly do you want to know, Nigel?" Joel asked in tones less peremptory than those of his colleague and with a respectful attitude that Nigel interpreted as a polite way of putting himself in the place of someone younger.

"I know that you are conducting research on African landfills on behalf of a non-profit organisation," Nigel answered. "It is true?"

"Yes, that's true," Joel replied. "We returned from Accra a few days ago, after data collection in the Agbogbloshie landfill."

"I've read a lot about this place," Nigel interrupted.

"Okay, but it's not just what you see on a website. It is important to understand what goes on around landfills."

"I'm listening." Nigel was beginning to like this boy who was certainly showing more tact than Kurt, who was strangely silent and scrutinising him carefully.

"Every year, between twenty and fifty million tons of e-waste, or rather technological devices, are produced. These are devices which have previously been sold in the EU at a cost that also includes a 'recycling fee' for the regular disposal of the material."

"Up to this point everything seems clear to me," said Nigel.

"Yes, if that tax was actually used for such 'recycling'," Kurt said.

Joel waited a moment before continuing the conversation, as if unsure whether Kurt meant to continue. Then he carried on: "Despite the four billion euros obtained through the disposal tax, two-thirds of technological waste never reaches an approved plant." Joel took a short break to sip his coffee. The more he talked, the more Nigel began to understand that he was the real analyst, the more studious and reflective of the two, whereas Kurt was the man of action and direction.

"Is this where Africa's landfills come into play?" Nigel asked.

"Exactly. Recycling a computer in Germany, or a monitor in

France, costs around three and a half to five euros. In Ghana, it doesn't cost more than a euro and a half. This is how the game is played."

"I don't understand though; if the material is sent to Africa to be recycled, how are the landfills formed?" asked Nigel.

"It's simple," Kurt said. "Think of the hundreds of containers from the United States, Great Britain, Belgium, Holland, Spain and Denmark, that fill the docks of African ports such as Tema (the largest in the Ghana) every month. Think of the hundreds of tons of used technology products inside these containers. Think of a good portion of the material, between 25% and 75%, that is not reusable. Where do you think this material ends up? It gets piled up in huge landfills."

"And the houses of the locals are near these dumps," added Nigel, remembering what he had read on the internet.

"Homes? Whole neighbourhoods, villages," Joel exclaimed, "which become one with the dumps! Populations that live, sleep, eat and work on garbage. Children play among pieces of metal and plastic and work among this waste."

"With devastating damage to all of us sooner or later," Kurt pressed. "Here we are not talking only about the countries affected and exploited by this system. We're talking about our planet and the lack of clean disposal that will harm everyone's lives."

"Excuse my naivety but is it possible that all this happens in silence, that there has never been an international reaction?" Nigel deliberately asked a trivial question, knowing he'd get more news from it.

"International reaction?" Kurt laughed. "Like that of governments which meet to denounce themselves and say they have to be good? Have you never heard of the Basel Convention?

It dates from 1989, not yesterday, as I'm sure you know. It forbids the international trafficking of toxic waste. What do you think the states did? Of course they signed it. All those from the EU and 182 others – apart from the United States, which is a major producer of e-waste and Haiti. Despite the prohibition, what do you think Western countries do? They use the excuse of donations and the claim of reducing the digital divide in developing countries to get rid of their old laptops. What more do you want? In this way they 'wipe their faces' by appearing to be benefactors towards the needy of the southern nations of the world and, at the same time, they make themselves popular with their own people, keeping them away from the crap they send straight to others instead. Brilliant, isn't it?"

"And what's the business angle on all this? In short, who earns, and how much?" Nigel asked.

"Someone certainly makes money, and probably a lot," Joel said. "The amount of waste arriving in Africa has increased tenfold in recent years and the illegal trafficking of toxic waste has already exceeded that of narcotics in terms of turnover. Furthermore, another important aspect must be considered: the low-cost labour available in large quantities in developing countries."

"You mean landfill labour? For what?"

"According to the International Labour Organisation, more than half of sub-Saharan Africa's urban workforce engages in informal activities, including landfills. In Ghana, the successive privatisations that began in the 1980s, the liberalisation of trade and the elimination of subsidies have led a large part of society to depend on the 'survival industry', and in this economic branch, work in landfills is particularly beneficial. At the Agbogbloshie landfill, there are at least five thousand people earning an average of three and a half dollars a day, almost double what the average informal worker can scrape together."

"Who works there?"

"Everyone. Young, old, men, women. Children."

The waitress's voice, bringing their receipt forced a pause in the conversation. For Nigel, Joel and Kurt's story was opening up a totally new aspect of a world which he had so far approached only for mere tourism. He had been to Africa many times, to see the beauty of nature and to discover something different. But it had always been about lovely things. He had not failed to come across hunger and filth and poverty, but he had always approached them with the typical detachment of someone who, partly out of scepticism and partly out of cowardice, is convinced that reality will never change that much.

"Many of the people who work at the Agbogbloshie landfill," Joel continued, "come to Accra from the Muslim north of the country, the poorest part of Ghana and the part most affected by inter-ethnic violence. Since 2000, when the landfill started working, it has become a refuge for many of them, and at the same time a place where they can find the means to survive. Whole families, children, adults, the elderly."

"But what are they doing?"

"Most of them mine motherboards, aluminium and copper and then resell them to metal traders."

"And they live off this?"

"And they get sick from it!" Kurt pointed out bitterly, speaking again. "They live in the garbage in the open and everywhere. The waste blocks the water currents of the lagoon and pollutes the aquifers of the Odaw River, with all the consequent damage to the biodiversity of the Korle Lagoon, on which the landfill is located. Not to mention the catastrophic effects on the human organism: the concentration of lead in the soil exceeds that allowed by international standards by a thousand percent. Furthermore, workers are continuously exposed to toxic substances such as mercury, brominated flame retardants or cadmium. The accumulation of these substances in the body produces irreversible disabling diseases in the medium and long term: headaches, coughs, skin eruptions, involuntary abortions, problems with the reproductive system and various types of tumours."

Rarely had Nigel's attention been focused on something with such intensity as at that moment.

"How is it possible that all this—"

"How is it possible that all this exists?" Kurt finished Nigel's sentence. "How is it possible that the ground of Agbogbloshie is covered in plastic and metal debris, that it is increasingly black, more polluted, more inert, more and more covered by the columns of smoke from burnt rubbish? That rubbish of electrical cables is burnt by kids, children, in makeshift bonfires to extract copper. Nigel, I've been wondering that for years."

Joel interrupted Kurt and resumed his speech in a slower and less passionate tone, more technical and less personal.

"The technological junk industry plays a fundamental role in Ghana: at least thirty thousand people make their living from this business, which contributes around two hundred million dollars to the country's economy. Despite this, or perhaps because of the economic impact of tech junk, the Ghanaian parliament has never legislated to regulate its importation. But it's not just a Ghanaian problem, because if the northern hemisphere applied its own protocols, the problem probably wouldn't exist. But rich countries have no interest in solving it due to the high costs it would entail. So even if Ghana decides to change something, it won't be able to do much on its own."

"And what can be done then?" Nigel asked with an impetuousness that surprised himself. A moment of silence fell.

"It depends on what each of us wants. You, Nigel, why did you want to know all this? For your radio piece?" Kurt asked looking at his interlocutor with his black and piercing eyes. Silence again. "Do you really want to do a real investigation? Or do you simply want to present a series of facts that you can find on the internet?"

"What do you mean?"

"I mean that if you want to do a real job, you have to begin to understand the lives of those people as much as possible. Otherwise, you will give your listeners a nice radio package, filled with data, estimates and international mission statements. It won't be a waste of time, but instead, you could tell people something that they really need to know, make them feel the importance of your every single word. Maybe they won't give you the Pulitzer, but at least no one will be able to say you haven't acted as a journalist."

Again, that brazen tone was irritating, but Nigel was beginning to see Kurt as a man of great passions and ideals and even feel a kind of envy for him. In the face of this insistence on how to do, or not to do, a news report that could reach people's hearts, he wondered if Kurt hadn't once been a reporter himself. But perhaps he just wanted the widest possible circulation for what he believed to be the real news.

"Kurt, Joel, take my curiosity away. I'm sure what you say is all true. I trust you. But have you verified that our waste actually ends up in African landfills? What is this trade in e-waste? I know that I have always dealt with music, but precisely because I am a journalist, I have to be sure that we are talking about something that has actually been confirmed. You've introduced yourself as an industry expert, and have just returned from Accra after a data collection. What data?"

"Then you really want to do your piece?" Kurt smiled. "Of course we did some research."

"Which is?"

"We built a lot on what others have already done," Joel said. "In practice, about a year ago we equipped four disused computers with chips and threw them in the landfills of four different European cities. The chips allowed us to follow them throughout their journey."

"But how was that possible? This is high tech!" exclaimed Nigel.

"And you think we can't, huh?" Kurt replied. "Instead, we have to surprise you. It's all legal what we did and, yes, high tech; but not impossible."

"Okay, so what did you find out?"

"Well, the four computers went the way I was telling you about," Joel said. "They sailed from four different European ports in containers and arrived at the Port of Tema, Ghana, from where they were distributed to different places. Two ended up in a thrift shop and two in the Agbogbloshie dump. They are still intact there."

"And of course all of this is documented, isn't it?"

"Certainly. In a few days the report will be released in which we will disclose the life of our 'infiltrator' computers. For this, we have just returned from Accra. An acquaintance of ours, who has also returned, is our contact who is dealing with the most disturbing aspect of the matter, that is the health of the inhabitants of the Agbogbloshie landfill. Meeting her could be useful for your piece."

"I'd love that."

"Well, now you know the story, and you can have the data tomorrow too. It's all up to you now."

"Let me have the documents."

Agbogbloshie, November 25

Nelson, Kofi, Ama, Martin, Palletta, Nii, Aziz and Osagyefo had also been listening to the Baba the night before, and this morning they were sleepier than usual on their way to the white sorceress. But they were wide awake in the afternoon when they arrived at Nelson's uncle's warehouse.

Nelson had carved out a space for himself, a personal realm cluttered with things he had found in the landfill that had intrigued him or that he had deemed of possible future use. He had managed to rearrange an old and battered battery-operated tape recorder, and he could hear cassettes which he also found in the rubbish.

For a few weeks only, he had some recordings of David Bowie. Father Angelo had told him who the singer was, but he knew nothing about Bowie. To Nelson, this was just the voice of a man thousands of miles away from where he slept, lived, played and worked. But Bowie had become a friend to him. And when Nelson listened to *Life on Mars*, for him, it was like climbing on a star moving towards an infinite and distant space, lulled by Bowie's voice.

Some scholars and geneticists argue that everyone has innate intellectual gifts. If true, Nelson's brain cells contained all the genes of an electrical engineer; he was already in swaddling clothes, and anyone who saw him tinkering in that warehouse would have been convinced of it. This was an unlikely hypothesis, however, because Nelson was possessive of what he called his 'workshop'. All the children knew of its existence, but very few had entered it. Today's general exception had been inspired by an event that concerned them all: the imminent departure of the sorceress. It had come naturally, but now it frightened him a little. He feared that his most intimate reasons for joy would not remain the same once he shared them with others.

"Nelson, but this place is wonderful!" Martin exclaimed as he crossed its threshold for the first time.

Everyone looked curiously at the tools arranged in order on a worktable. Ama didn't understand the meaning of that room or the purpose of those tools, but she was happy about it anyway because it was as if she were in another landfill, all clean and tidy. Kofi, who had been there before, concentrated on the items Nelson had collected and refurbished. They seemed ready to be sold in one of the downtown stores. And who knew? Maybe one day the first electronics store in their neighbourhood would be born in that warehouse. He wished this for Nelson sincerely, even though he knew that his friend didn't dream like that; instead, he dreamed of Mars.

"Come, I'll show you the computer that we can give to the sorceress. I didn't find this one in the landfill; Father Angelo gave it to me when I told him what I needed it for."

Nelson pulled a rectangular black and silver object from under the table. It was similar to the ones children found in the dump every morning and collected for their work, but this one was shiny and looked new. "Now there's no electricity, but I have already charged the battery for a while. I think that's enough."

"What does it mean to 'charge the battery'?" Osagyefo asked.

"Look, you get electricity with this special wire, here."

Nelson showed him. "You see? On the one hand it plugs into the socket, and on the other hand there's this little piece that fits into this hole in the computer. Current is poured into it, and for a while the computer works even if it is disconnected from the electric socket."

The object looked like a book. Or a door. Nelson opened it, pressed a button and a small light appeared on the screen, then a series of strange writings, until he pressed another key and the screen turned blank. The children watched him dumbfounded. They knew what it was. They knew what the objects they collected at the landfill were for. They knew about Nelson's tape recorder. Yet they thought that those objects, the computers, the CD players like Father Angelo's, the speakers that amplified music and voices, the cell phones that not only the recoveries but also many inhabitants of Agbogbloshie had, could only work when new, or at most when they were fixed in specialised centres in the city. Those from the landfill were only used for the pieces which could be resold.

"Nelson, how did you do it? It works!" Kofi asked breaking everyone's silence of amazement.

"Is it magic?" Osagyefo asked.

Nelson smiled proudly. "I did some jobs, little stuff. Now I'll show you better. Look here, with this keyboard I can write anything I want on the screen." He pressed the 'b' key and a 'b' appeared on the screen; then the 'e', the 'l' and the 'o' twice. The word 'beautiful' formed on the screen.

Ama bent down to look under the table.

"What are you doing, Ama?" Palletta asked her.

"I just wanted to see if anyone under the table was writing the letters that Nelson presses on the keyboard."

"It's useless for you to search! It all happens inside this box here," explained Nelson.

"But then... you can write without pen and paper?" Ama's eyes widened in wonder.

"Exactly, without the pen and paper. And you can also read it again, because everything you write can be saved with a keystroke, and when you want you can go and reread it, look!" he explained, pressing another key and making the writing 'd..id bowie' appear.

"The 'a' and 'v' are missing," Nii pointed out.

"Yes, some letters on the keyboard still need to be sorted out. But it's trivial stuff. I understand the mechanism. Now I'll turn off the computer and show you how to do it," Nelson said.

But first the children saw him erase the letters on the screen one by one, by pressing another key.

"But this is magic!" insisted Osagyefo.

"Yes, it's a great spell for a sorceress," Nelson conceded, growing prouder.

"Do you think that where these computers come from, children like us can use them and do their homework at school? Think, what a treat! Not having to rewrite everything for a mistake!" Palletta was fascinated.

At that point the screen started flashing and went off by itself.

"That was you?" asked Aziz.

"No," said Nelson, "It has run out of charge."

"Then we can do nothing more?"

"Don't worry. We don't need electricity now. We have to open the keyboard, clean it well and reattach the keys properly."

And he set to work with everyone else around. Nothing had detracted from their enthusiasm.

"Doesn't the sorceress already have a computer?"

After all, it didn't matter that much. It didn't matter if the sorceress was already using that spell. What counted was that extraordinary moment, the fascinating mechanism they were discovering. It was important that they were doing it together. And doing it as a gift.

The children only left when they realised that their mothers were probably already on their way to call them to dinner. They passed a group of men arguing animatedly, without stopping. Kofi and Ama saw their father, but they didn't stop either, seeing that he was busy. They entered the house, and their mother told them to eat and go to bed right away.

"Your father is talking to your friends' fathers. He will be back shortly and will come to give you the blessing of the evening. Go now."

"We saw him," Kofi confirmed. "They meet every evening. What are they talking about?"

"The landfill. But you don't have to worry about it."

"Why? What are they going to do with the landfill?"

"Father Angelo says it is hurting us, but I don't know any more. The men are talking about it, but now you must eat, and then go to sleep because tomorrow you have to wake up early."

After dinner, the children undressed and lay down on either side of Samia who was already asleep.

"Kofi? Have you seen how many stars there are tonight?"

"Yes, and they are beautiful."

"Do you believe that we too have a star that protects us as the Baba told us?"

"I'm certain."

"And do you think my star will help me make my dreams come true?"

"Love, you will become a princess and dance in beautiful

dresses and with jewels on your arms and around your neck, like the ones you see in the junkyard magazines."

Ama felt a warm, silent tear roll down her cheek. She turned her back on her brother and turned her face towards the window which was open to the sky and dotted with stars. She cuddled the donkey to herself, managing only to say: "Thanks, Kofi."

London, December 7

"Is this the report that's coming out?" Nigel asked.

"Yes, and it's still under embargo, so you can't make it public until December 11," Kurt answered.

"Well, that's the date of my broadcast."

They had chosen to meet for the second time in the park below the radio headquarters. It was a small park that was always busy at any time of day. In the mornings, dog owners took their four-legged friends for a walk, at lunchtime the employees of the surrounding offices sat on the benches in their suits and ties and ate sandwiches from bags or, for the more health-conscious, dug wooden forks into salads in small plastic containers. The afternoon was filled, however, with boys and girls, accompanied by their mothers or babysitters, who poured into the play area with its slides, swings, a plastic castle and a sandpit where the little ones rolled on the ground while playing with marbles. A little further on, there was a short circular track where budding skaters enjoyed themselves for hours, circling and chasing each other.

It was six p.m., perhaps the finest hour, thought Nigel, with the light of the sun already set behind the horizon which continued to illuminate the last moments of the day, for those that were anticipating the evening.

He loved that time of day when the hustle and bustle gave way to calm. As a child, he too went with his mother to the playground near his home in Wimbledon, where he had grown up. It was there that he gave vent to all his exuberance, playing with the other children, some lifelong friends, others, one-day friends. His mother also brought him chocolate chip cookies, his favourite, in a snack basket with a picture of Snoopy on it. He had been crazy about those biscuits; there was not a day when he didn't trade one or two for the other children's football cards. And his afternoons were spent between games and snacks in that park until his mother stopped chatting with the other mothers and told him to collect all the toys and say goodbye to his friends. "We'll be back tomorrow anyway," she reassured him. And it was true; the next day, they came back.

Maybe he didn't realise it at the time, but he also loved that walk, with the backpack on his shoulders, hand in hand with his mother, along the road that took them home from the park. At that hour the drugstore was still open and Mr O'Brien, the proprietor of Irish descent, came out of the shop to say hello. "Hello, little one, come in. Mary has something to give you," he said, stroking Nigel's face. Mary was Mr O Brien's wife, small and chubby like him, with a smile that made people happy just to see her. She looked like a female copy of her husband, except for the long red moustache. She cooked very well, and gave her best in the preparation of desserts, which she made into real little works of art, decorating them with flowers, animals or objects, in coloured marzipan and enriched with small sugar candies.

Every day, Nigel went to the drugstore window to admire them. It wasn't so much the desire to eat them as the joy they aroused in him. However, Mary knew that, like any child, Nigel would never say no to one of her sweets, and so it had become a habit to have a small package ready with one of the day's delights when he returned from the park with his mother. He always remembered the little pat that the woman gave him on the cheek as he approached to give her a kiss, delivered with a cheerful and kind smile.

Then, with his sweets in his trouser pocket, he gave his little hand back to his mother, and together they resumed their journey home. As he walked, he told her about his games with his friends, and also the quarrels and the bad words that, by mistake or out of temporary anger, had passed between them. That moment was just for the two of them and it was another of the best memories that he kept.

"It's all written down, right?" he asked Kurt, returning his focus to why he was there.

"Sure, everything. From the beginning, when we put the chips in the four computers, to the end, and the fates that befell them. As I told you, we're not the first to go the electrical route like this. And the results were the ones we have already illustrated. Of those four computers, two are now in the junkyard and two in a second-hand electronics store in Accra."

"Second-hand shop?"

"Exactly. The streets of Accra are filled with second-hand household appliance and electronics stores, such as televisions, computers, printers, irons and telephones. Just think, some refrigerators still bear their original stickers or labels that mark their origin, all of them from the Northern hemisphere."

"But do these products have a market?"

"Do they have a market? African technicians, called the 'black geeks', work inside these shops. They are the ones who repair everything that arrives and then put it back on the market. Much of the technological material circulating in Ghana, from mobile phones to computers, is supplied by second-hand markets. And this is not entirely negative, if you think of all the families, offices and businesses that can make use of it in this way."

"Well, that sounds like a good thing. But how long does each of these tools last?"

"Bingo, brother!"

Nigel was struck by that 'brother' from Kurt. So far, he hadn't said anything that might have seemed like an opening to some complicity between them.

"Most of the electronic devices have already been used for a long time so, even once they are resold on the used market, they may last for a few weeks, or a few months, at most a year. After that, however, they go back to the landfills, together with all the other broken iron that is unusable, even second-hand, and are thrown away directly."

"And then, would it still be considered foreign-produced e-waste?"

"No. It would be seen as locally produced waste... Do you understand the trick now?"

"You told me there has already been some research to confirm this, right?"

"Yes, what I'm telling you is not a scoop, because everything has already been established and is widely known. Except that it is not talked about much, even though it is disgusting exploitation that is affecting the health of the local inhabitants."

"Explain better."

"As I told you, one of our representatives worked there, a doctor who is specialising in the effects of e-waste material on human health. We wanted to ascertain the consequences of this accumulation of rubbish on all those who live around the landfills. And for five months, our friend carried on her research also thanks to a university grant."

"But is it there for you or for the university?"

"When you have a passion for the well-being of others in your heart, there is no title for which you do it. However, she went there on her own for the university, and our activities crossed paths. You will write a part of the report, obviously not in scientific detail, but clearly enough to make people understand the real situation."

"I'd like to meet her."

"Of course, I already proposed it yesterday. I'll set you up with a meeting. Our searches were concentrated in Agbogbloshie, a district of the city of Accra, inhabited by thousands of people between hovels, muddy roads and heaps of scrap e-waste. It is here that many recover, weigh, transport and resell pieces made from metals."

"Okay, you also told me this yesterday—"

"What I didn't tell you is that Agbogbloshie has turned into a cemetery of abandoned plastics and household appliances. And to think that once upon a time it was a green and radiant area." A sigh accompanied Kurt's words, and his expression betrayed anger at a vanished world that he had certainly known.

"Are these materials that have a negative effect on the health of the neighbourhood population?"

"Yes, but not only because they are piled up in the landfill. The boys, called 'e-waste boys', burn tons of electric cables to extract the copper and then sell it for a few cedis, the local currency, per kilo. They do it because they live in conditions of extreme poverty, and in order not to starve, they try to survive in this way. Without a mask, their lungs are filled with all the toxic fumes. Do you have any idea what this means? Aluminium, lead and copper fill the bodies of these boys: many of them fall ill with cancer and die. And that's not all. The fumes rise into the sky, poison the air, fall back on the ground and end up in the plants and animal foods, animals and plants which the inhabitants eat, in their blood, in the urine, in their mothers' milk. This is real contamination and real genocide."

"But if everything is so well known and discussed why is no initiative taken? How is it possible that the government ignores it, even in the face of complaints from humanitarian associations? I saw that there are quite a few—"

"There are many complaints. In reality, the government has tried to react but in the wrong way. They sent bulldozers to clear the drains, but they actually demolished part of the city, leaving thousands of people homeless. This is not the solution – if you demolish the houses, others will be built for the same reasons as the previous ones were – and the problem has merely moved."

It was getting dark, and the mothers were starting to leave the park with their children. The voices of the women calling for toys to be put back mingled with the cries of the children who continued to play and laugh with each other. Who knew if anyone had watched him and his mother with the same nostalgia? Suddenly Nigel smiled.

"Incredible," he said, "just three days ago I was exclusively involved in music and now... here I am talking to a social rights activist about landfills, children, hunger, poverty... Who would have thought it?"

"Does it make you smile so much, Nigel?"

"No, not at all. Take it easy. It just makes me think."

"About what?"

"About nothing specifically, except about the general rule that life is not always what you control.

"True, but you can always start becoming the protagonist if you want to."

"Yes, of course, my partner and all our busy friends like you tell me this too, Kurt. The truth is that I don't believe much in what we, single and ordinary mortals, can do. Everything is in the hands of those who manage the lobbies and financial centres who, in turn, manage each of us."

"Then why are we here? Why are you wasting your time with me and with what is happening in the landfills?"

"For my work... I was asked to do a piece and I'm trying to do it in the best possible way."

"Edifying—"

"No, it's not edifying... Maybe you're right. But it doesn't mean that because you activists put your soul and heart into it, it must be the same for everyone. I admit it: I don't wave and I don't yearn. I'm certainly sorry about everything you're telling me. But having said that, after speaking with you, I return to my thoughts, to my home, to my partner. In all honesty, my first concern is how to make the best of my life, have a secure job that will allow me to live, and ensure a peaceful old age. Petty? Think what you like, but I don't think I should be damned for that."

Kurt listened to him without replying, perhaps beginning to develop the conviction that what he was hearing wasn't entirely true of Nigel.

"Tell me just one thing. Will you make our story public in your service? Our searches? Are you going to do the report on the dump revealing everything?"

"I'll read the report tonight. You organise me an in with the doctor."

"Okay, you'll get the report and the meeting with the doctor. But meanwhile, think about what you say makes you so happy. Is it really enough for you, as you say?"

The two parted with a quick handshake, and without saying anything else. Nigel walked home, going back to watching the children with their mothers, experiencing strong feelings of joy and security he had felt at their age. At that moment, he rediscovered the desire to go back, to touch once again the smooth skin of his mother's hand, to talk to her with that same spontaneity that he had lost over the years, to feel the scent that enveloped him every time he embraced her – the iris perfume she wore every morning before leaving the house to take him to school. He wasn't melancholy, but the joy of perceiving those moments as an adult, were so distant yet so alive. Almost without realising it, his thoughts went to the children in the dump, to what their moments of play and complicity with their parents could be like.

All children play, he thought, *and all children think their world is universal. Who knows what the universe of children from the landfill is like?*

The darkness of the evening accompanied his thoughts along the noisy street from the traffic at the end of the day, illuminated by the lights of the shops and clubs.

Agbogbloshie, November 26

The children were returning from their morning meeting with their sorceress.

"So, children, you heard another story from the Baba last night, didn't you?"

"Yes, Father Angelo. But is old grandfather like Jesus?" asked Osagyefo who was a Christian.

"No, Osagyefo," Ama ruled, "the Baba is not Jesus, but he is someone who speaks directly to Jesus because he is the best and wisest of all of us, like Father Angelo."

"Well, both Baba and I try to get closer to God's will and do our best. Jesus told us to do it. You know, even if you don't see him, he is always close to all of us and always loves us."

"But what if he's dead?" Ama asked.

"It is true, he is dead, but in reality, he continues to live and to be always present."

"But how? If he's dead, he's dead!" Nelson retorted.

"No, it's not like that," Aziz said. "The spirits of ancestors and unborn children also lived in my grandfather's village. I used to live there too, but I don't remember it well."

"Children, do you remember hearing me say that Jesus came back to life three days after his death?"

"But then Jesus is a spirit, like that of the ancestors of my grandfather's village?"

"Not exactly. He rose again with his body and is now alive forever," explained the priest, who was annoyed with himself for starting that conversation, especially with children who weren't all Christians. And even with the others, it was certainly not yet the time to face the central dogma of Christianity, a truth that can only be accepted in faith.

But 'Little Miss Why' didn't let go: "And why can't we see him then?"

"We will see him at the end of our lives. And if we've lived well, death won't be as bad a thing as we all fear."

"So, if today I am good and tonight I die, will I see Jesus?"

"Not tonight, Ama. For you, for all of you, there is still a lot of time." Then Father Angelo looked at the smoke rising in the distance from the dump and a sharp pain in his soul reminded him that it was not true. "Do you want to sing a nice song now?"

"Yes, shall we sing the one about the sky?" Osagyefo yelled excitedly at the idea.

"Very well, then let's sing it together, but without shouting too much… we don't want to wake everyone up, do we?"

"*Volare… ohhohh… ohhohh… nel blue dipinto di blue… felice di essere lassu… e volavo volavo felice più in alto del sole…*"

The success of Domenico Modugno's song, *Volare*, the most famous in the world, had been liked by his boys more than he liked it. He had taught them, above all, because it was easy to learn and remember. And he was sorry that he hadn't had as much luck with *Volta la Carta*, the only song by his favourite Fabrizio De André which he had deemed suitable for children and which he continually tried to teach them, despite the difficulties of the text in a much more articulate Italian.

Hearing them sing and singing with them, Father Angelo felt the pain leave his chest, as if he wanted to convince himself that their vitality was stronger than the threat; as if he were one of them too and the only thing to remember from visits to the sorceress were the breakfasts with biscuits and milk, all eight sitting around the table in the back room of the one used as a laboratory. He knew that the reason they had to go to that house was still not clear to the children. But he saw them erasing every doubt and perplexity, and every residue of sleep, in the pleasure of dipping those coconut biscuits in glasses full of fresh milk. Those breakfasts were a luxury they weren't used to in their own homes.

And he knew that their vitality soon erased any veil of melancholy or suffering. Besides, they didn't often have any and they never lasted long. Life has a strange alchemy; those children deprived of everything, other than a few recycled toys, such as Ama's little donkey brought in from some charitable association, were always happy.

It didn't take much – just an old ball or a truck wheel – to see them rejoicing in an improvised soccer match or a botched swing. And Father Angelo wondered once again how those children of a world immersed in the most absolute poverty could maintain that candour and cleanliness that he scarcely found in the world from which he came.

At the back of the line, Aziz had stopped singing and had slowed his pace to a stop, breathing more and more heavily.

"What's happening to you?" Father Angelo asked.

"What's the matter?" his companions echoed, crowding round.

"I'm fine, I'm fine... I just feel very tired," said Aziz, feebly.

"Calm down, children, calm down. It's nothing." The priest tried to reassure them by lifting Aziz in his arms. "Eh, little rascal, isn't that an excuse for me to take you home? Come into my arms, for today you have a nice discount voucher!"

The line had dissolved. They all went grouped around Father Angelo and Aziz, to stay close to him and to caress his bare feet and calves.

It was Ama again who broke the silence: "Father, Aziz has been more and more tired lately. He has to ask his mum to let him sleep more."

"Okay, I'll tell her, don't worry." But worry was the expression on his face.

"We too are tired. And sometimes even Kofi has trouble breathing at night like Aziz has now."

"That is not true!"

"Yes, it is! You wake up suddenly in the night, and I feel like you can't breathe for a while."

"Woe to you if you tell Mum!"

"Good." Father Angelo called them to order. "Kofi, is it true that you have these difficulties at night?"

"It is true, but only for a few days. Please, Father Angelo, don't say anything to Mum because otherwise she won't let me play football anymore."

The priest's white head nodded. He wouldn't have said anything to Abenà that she didn't already know. It would only renew the painful thoughts of damage she could not avoid.

"Father Angelo, why are some of us not well? Is that why we go to the sorceress, to ward off the evil eye that is on us?" Nelson asked.

"Evil eye? Who put these ideas into your head?"

"I hear the grown-ups. They say a sorcerer made black magic and that all children will be affected."

"No, boys, no evil eye has hit you. However, it happens that people can feel unwell in life. And then, do you know what 'the evil eye' is?"

"It's when someone wants you to feel bad, and then they concentrate and pray for it," Palletta replied.

"And you think that would be enough to make a person feel bad? Could evil be stronger than good? However, if you think so, you must turn to your God to help you overcome what you are experiencing negatively, such as illness."

"And does he help you?" Ama asked.

"God gives us strength to face the obstacles we encounter in life. You have to talk to Him and ask Him for help. Entrust yourselves to Him and, with the strength that He instils in you, face every small or big obstacle you encounter in life."

"But then we do not go to the sorceress for the evil eye?" pressed Martin, not too convinced.

"Of course not! And... tell me, what else have you heard from adults about the sorceress?"

"Some say that the sorceress will only bring harm because she will prevent children from working and helping families with the money they earn. But others say that instead she will help us," replied Palletta.

"Yes, I've heard the same things too!" Kofi confirmed.

"And you, children, what do you think of the sorceress?"

"She's good to us," Nii said. "It's a bit tiring to go to her early in the morning when everyone is asleep, but she always gives us sweets and milk. But I still don't understand what all those things she does are for. And why can't we tell others about it?"

"And above all, the recuperators mustn't know," Nelson added. "But why, Father Angelo?"

"The sorceress wants only your good and the good of your friends. But not everyone understands this, and most think instead that she just wants to prevent you from making money from the landfill."

"But why can't we go at a time of day better than early in the morning?" Kofi asked.

"Because in this way you all have a nice breakfast together," the priest cut him short, smiling.

They arrived Aziz's house. The children stopped outside, and Father Angelo went through the open door with the little boy asleep in his arms. The child's mother and grandfather barely had time to mechanically pronounce the *salam aleikum* when dismay and excitement appeared on their faces.

"What happened, Father Angelo?" the woman asked.

"*Wa alaikoum assalam*. Don't worry, he's just very tired and now he needs to rest." He handed the child into his mother's arms and went out into the street. "Go home, children, and get ready for school. Aziz will be well soon, rest assured."

Aziz's grandfather had followed him, and he too waved a little greeting and a little reassurance to the children who were leaving. But he didn't hold back his anguish: "What should we do? Aziz is getting worse and worse. He keeps losing weight and can no longer breathe well," he asked the priest, the foreigner who had come from afar without leaving immediately, as if he who had remained among them to help them could have every answer.

"Now the most important thing is to let him rest. Then we'll deal with everything else. One breath at a time. His pain is enough for each day," replied Father Angelo placing his hand on the old man's shoulder.

And the priest walked away with his tangle of conflicting thoughts. The lives of the children made cheerful by an old Italian song. The death that made clear its assaults on little Aziz. The blatant waste that fuelled the poisonous landfill. The absolute misery that was the price of that waste.

And all this confirmed the intuition he had had many years earlier: there are places where poverty and suffering are such as to not allow words to express them. One can only live with them to try and alleviate them.

London, December 8

Like any other major western capital, London takes on a special magic during Christmas. The streets wear glittering decorations. The shop windows are transformed into imaginary and fantastic polar villages with large Santa Claus puppets surrounded by reindeers, elves, teddy bears, and sleds ready to launch on the snow and into the sky. Silver threads of light cover entire facades of buildings like cascades of diamonds. In the cafés, fake fir branches surround billboards advertising hot chocolate and special cappuccino, served exclusively for the season.

Christmas, or rather, the days before, always brought about a feverish cheer in Nigel, between aperitifs, dinners with friends and frantic searches for gifts in the shops of Regent Street and Oxford Street. He liked all of it, and not even the protests of consumerism could make him feel guilty. He liked to stop at the Café Royal for his favourite treat, the chocolate brownie with hazelnut cream, a specialty of the Christmas season, even though Judith teased him for such a habit, typical of "ladies and gentlemen of good society."

On the other hand, the 25th was, in the warm atmosphere of the house, a lazy and sleepy day filled with Walt Disney films and cartoons on television, with their feel-good feelings and ever-positive endings. "Besides, isn't this Christmas;" he repeated to Judith every year, "the opportunity to regress for a few days into our childhood and relive what was the warmest and most magical thing we experienced without realising it?" And Judith knew he was right.

That December 8, they had woken up early. Nigel had the coffee maker and cups ready, while Judith had already put the eggs and bacon into the skillet with butter. It wasn't raining and the day promised to be beautiful and sunny, albeit cold. When the phone rang, they had just begun to agree on the program for the day: a Caravaggio exhibition at the National Gallery, a tour of Regent Street, and a nice bergamot tea with the chocolate brownie and hazelnut cream at the Café Royal.

"Hello, Nigel." It was Gareth.

"Hi. Good to hear from you, how are you?" Nigel was pleased to hear from his friend.

"Everything's fine; you? I hope I'm not disturbing you at this hour?"

"No, we were having breakfast. Tell me everything."

"Tatiana and I are taking the brats to the toy parade. Do you want to come? That way at least we can manage to spend some time together. In the last few months, we've been a bit lost... You know, the children alternately went down with the flu, and then Tatiana and I got sick too."

"Yes, Judith told me that she's been talking to Tatiana. I'd love to see you. But where is the toy parade? Still on Regent Street, right?"

"Yes, always."

"Hang on, I can hear Judith... no, she understood what we were saying and she's signalling that it's okay with her."

"Perfect! Let's meet at eleven in Piccadilly Circus and then we'll go together?"

"Piccadilly Circus at eleven. We'll be there!" Nigel repeated, catching Judith's agreement.

"Well! Later then."

The end of the call was accompanied by the muttering of coffee on the hob. Even at home, he preferred the mocha to pods or the kettle, and for this reason his closest friends called him 'the Italian'.

"It'll be nice to see Gareth and Tatiana. I've heard from you a lot these past few weeks and we kept talking about meeting up," said Judith, serving the bacon and eggs.

"I'm very pleased too. Gareth is one of the dearest friends I have. I've known him since the first year of high school... wow, a lifetime!"

"Do you want toast?"

"Thanks, wait while I get the butter." Opening the fridge, Nigel gave a satisfied smile: "Salted butter! My favourite! I adore you! We haven't had it in a while."

"You're right. I have to say that I'm starting to like it too, despite my diet." Judith smiled. "Gareth is a really nice person. And I get along well with Tatiana too. I would say that she has fully integrated here in London."

"Where is she from? I know she's South American, but where exactly from?"

"She's from Chile. I think she's also a good architect, although she's decided not to look for work for now. Those rowdy children absorb her completely." Judith rolled her eyes.

"Well, like Gareth was as a kid! Thomas is six and David two, isn't he?"

"Wow, Nigel, for a man who doesn't want to have kids, you're really good at remembering the details of your friends' kids!"

"Well, I bet you know their birthdays too!"

"Of course I know. And you know why? You're godfather to Thomas, so it's important that I remember both of their birthdays!

And we're always invited to their birthday parties."

"We certainly don't go for Tatiana's buttercream pies," Nigel observed with a sigh of disgust, and both of them laughed at the thought of having to digest even a single teaspoon of those sweets. They were certainly beautiful, brightly coloured and covered with smarties and various decorations, but for them it remained one of the many mysteries of childhood to understand how those cakes, so heavy for adults, were so loved by children and digested by their little stomachs.

Nigel didn't want children of his own, but he was happy with those of others "as long as it was for a few hours." And he was already anticipating the joy of holding Thomas on his shoulders to show him the toy parade. And Judith, who knew him, had seen it on his face, even as he spoke to Gareth. When he was with Thomas, or with the children of other friends of theirs, he became a child among them, indeed perhaps the most childlike of all. He didn't let them play; he played with them. And Judith was increasingly thinking that his reticence about fatherhood was really a fear of taking responsibility.

Agbogbloshie, November 26

Perhaps it was from seeing Aziz sick, or perhaps because the air was hotter and damper and more pressing that day, that the children moved listlessly and very slowly in the dump. Their hands rummaged through the electronic wires and the wreckage as if in slow motion. Even Nelson, always ready to jump from one point to another to find new pieces to sell or to keep for himself, was clearly disinterested in everything. Ama was diverted by the pages of another old magazine found in the landfill.

It was the second time this had happened to her, and she thought it was something splendid. She understood that the women portrayed had something special. After all, Father Angelo only took photographs in important circumstances. But she didn't understand the clothes of the girls he photographed even if, they were beautiful. Ama wondered if the Prince of England would like her if she was dressed like this, in very short skirts and low-cut blouses and with a dog tied to a leather rope, although it would probably be a goat or a cow that shouldn't get lost. But what amazed Ama most were the shoes. How could they walk with such high and pointed things on their feet? Something told her she should learn to do it too, for her prince, but how and where? Certainly not in the streets she walked every day and certainly not in the landfill.

That morning the seven children of the sorceress' party who were left now that Aziz wasn't there, wondered why their parents, despite the pennies they brought home, were less and less happy to know they were working in that place. Kofi and Ama's father came home from evening meetings with the other men increasingly worried, and the two little children understood that the cause was precisely the landfill itself. Even Father Angelo was against it and had tried to organise more lessons, more choirs and more football matches to keep them away.

But the children actually liked it. That huge pile of materials from other places wasn't just a way to get money. It was also a playing field and possibly a school. Sure, the computers were mostly broken, the cell phones wouldn't turn on, the refrigerators were just big chunks of rusty metal, and the radios and CD players were a tough challenge if they were to be restored, but they were all messages from different worlds, and without the dump they would have missed them.

And the children were fascinated. Everyone, not just Nelson, took something for themselves, something for their personal treasure troves, while looking for copper and other things to sell, and that was as important as the money obtained from the recuperators, from which their parents usually left them a small amount. Each child jealously guarded a few coins and banknotes in a small hiding place. In those houses which were only four walls and a precarious roof resting on the bare earth, this might be a box, a hole in the floor, or even inside one of their toys, like Ama's little donkey with its red saddle cloth.

Each one knew what he would do with those treasures when he got a little older. Kofi would have used them for a trip to Germany to meet the Bayern team whose photos he had seen in the magazines that the German gentleman from the 'humanitarian association' had shown him. Kofi had asked the German how to make his dream come true, and the man had promised him, hastily and without thinking, as is often done with children, that one day he would get him a plane ticket. But then he disappeared overnight. However, even if the promise had become worthless, Kofi's determination continued.

Ama wanted to buy herself a nice dress for meeting the Prince of England. She couldn't show up in her everyday cotton dress or even with the one she only wore to parties. This new magazine confirmed her choice. Perhaps the girls in the picture were from the same country as the prince – from the little she had learned, she understood that it was written in English – all had those strange clothes and straight hair. Black or white, the girls all looked the same, and Ama was starting to feel that she had to make herself like them.

Nii, Martin, and Palletta, on the other hand, had decided that one day they would go into partnership, and with the savings of all three, they would buy the right machines to make sweets, as they had told everyone, ever since they had found a sort of large kitchen utensil with 'Candy cooking' written on it, with moulds of various shapes for candy, amidst the toys abandoned in the landfill. To prove it, they had taken their find to Father Angelo and plugged it into the electricity. But it wouldn't turn on, so they promised each other that as soon as they had enough money, they'd buy a new one and open a candy store for the whole neighbourhood.

In the meantime, Aziz had decided to buy himself a real bed, one that he could have all to himself, not just when neither of his brothers were home.

The strangest idea – the most stratospheric in the true sense of the word, as Father Angelo would have said – was Nelson's: he wanted to build a missile, using all the material collected from the landfill that he had accumulated in the corner of his uncle's warehouse. But he didn't have the courage to tell anyone for fear that they would make fun of him. His dream was to go to Mars, the location of *Life on Mars*, his favourite song. Maybe there he would even meet David Bowie and they would sing together.

Only Osagyefo thought it would be more useful to use the money immediately, without waiting too long. As soon as he had any, he would go to Mama Bon's shop to buy his favourite lollipop, the one with the red paper that according to his father, was trying to imitate the taste of strawberries. And maybe doing this had really been a good investment.

Mama Bon, a tall woman with an alert and pleasant face, looked at him tenderly as soon as he entered the shop. "Today this lollipop is free for the youngest child who enters the shop first. And that is you. So take it but without saying anything to the others," was her habitual greeting. So Osagyefo would take the lollipop, put his usual and only dime back in his pocket and run away before another child entered.

It was Ama who broke the apathetic silence of that day. Impressed by the photo of a candy-pink dress worn by a girl who was walking a red carpet, she exclaimed: "This is the dress I want for when I meet the Prince of England!"

"Show us," Kofi urged.

"There it is! Look!"

"Yuck, girl stuff!" Palletta exclaimed.

"Stupid! I can wear it as I'm a girl and not a dude like you!"

"I think it should be shorter. How can you walk with all that stuff trailing behind?" Nii asked.

"*Uhmm*, maybe... but I like it. And I'm also going to wear these very high shoes."

"But who knows how much it will cost! You know how much money you will need?" Osagyefo asked.

"Of course, I know... but it's my dream," replied the little girl, but her voice was less bold and she lowered her chin to her chest.

"And you are right to have it, Ama! At least you won't grow up immediately," Kofi said.

The others looked at him, trying to understand the reason for his words, and the link that could exist between dreams and being adults. It was Osagyefo who explicitly asked him: "What do you mean?"

"It means that if we can dream, we can do it now, because we're still children and not adults."

"You mean adults don't dream?" Ama asked.

"I don't think so. They are too busy. Think of our parents; they are working all the time. In the evening, when we are all together, we hear them talking about the problems of the house and the money they need. When do you think they can dream? And what do they dream of? Nothing! They have before them only and always the same reality, day after day: the same commitments and the same worries."

"You're strange today, Kofi," Palletta commented.

"Yes, you make speeches we don't understand," Nii echoed.

"It's just that I don't really know how I feel either." Kofi tried to justify himself.

"To me, Kofi means that when you're a kid you can imagine anything because you still have to live the whole life that our parents lived," Nelson said. "But when do you stop being a child then? When do you stop dreaming?

"Perhaps when you no longer expect anything different," Kofi asserted, "when nothing surprises you anymore."

The others thought this was a phrase he had heard from adults or in some song. It was an unusual sentence in their daily speeches, one they didn't understand, but it aroused curiosity.

"Amazement is like… when you are happy about something, Kofi?" Ama asked.

"No, I think it's when you gasp when you see something beautiful. Like when you eat… I don't know, a candy you didn't think tasted so good. Adults have tasted everything and seen everything, so they are no longer surprised. They don't laugh and they don't cry anymore because they are used to everything and they are no longer surprised."

"Do you think our parents are no longer surprised by anything?" urged Ama.

"Perhaps. I never see Mum happy. She hardly ever smiles and seems to be bored all the time," Nelson observed.

"And we, on the other hand, are still amozed?" asked Osagyefo.

"Amazed, not amozed, Osagyefo," corrected Palletta.

"Anyway, I'm happy when the sun turns into a red fireball that throws itself into the sea while I wait for Dad to come back from fishing. Or when it rains so hard that you can collect water in a tub and put your feet in it. Instead, my mum and dad complain if it rains too hard or if it's too hot, and they are always discontented and thoughtful."

"A candy is enough for me to make me the happiest person in the world!" Osagyefo exclaimed.

"Imagine that. You settled for just one candy!" Palletta said.

"Of course, he's satisfied with a candy! He's not a fireball like you!" Ama rose up. "Listen to the princess who knows everything!"

"Let's go. Come on," said Kofi. "That's enough. We promised Father Angelo we wouldn't stay here too long."

Just as they came within sight of the house, Ama moved

away from the group. "You go on. I'll join you right away. I must go in for a moment."

"Everything okay?" Kofi asked her.

"Yes, I have to tell Mum something. But I'll be right there."

Ama found Abenà cooking and asked her in a rush, "Mum, do you still dream?"

Her mother looked at her, puzzled. Abenà remembered that, as a child, in the evening before falling asleep, she would look at the immense black space embellished with sparkling lights like so many jewels and choose one all for herself. She called it 'Stella Abenà', so no one could ever take it away from her. And she asked the star to transform her into one of the protagonists of the fairy tales her mother told her to put her to sleep: a queen or a gazelle. Later, when Abenà first saw an airplane flying over the village, she asked the star if she could be able to fly too, to find out what was beyond the horizon. But for a long time now, her dreams had been poorer and more concrete: a little less work for her husband, a few more things, above all, health for her children. She had learned to turn to God, but sometimes that star returned to her thoughts and helped her to recognise herself in every sigh of her little ones, as she saw them changing every day, understanding their every expression. And Abenà asked her star to ferry her prayers for her children to God, faster.

"Yes, I still dream, Ama, and I wish. I want you to grow up well and be strong and happy in life."

"But if you dream, Mother, you are still a child. Kofi says that it is children who dream, and when they become adults, they stop dreaming."

"Why did Kofi say that?"

"I don't know. We were talking about what I want to be when I grow up and what other people want to do. But none of us understood why Kofi said those things. And I don't understand what they mean."

"Maybe he doesn't know either."

"That's exactly what he said, Mum. Even he doesn't know why he said it."

"Don't think about it, and don't worry about him. Even if you don't believe it now, the truth is that you never stop dreaming. If that were the case, you would no longer be alive. The dream is something no one can take away from you. It belongs to you, it is with you always, and it accompanies you every day. Always."

London, December 8

They probably would have gone to the toy parade, regardless of Gareth's call. The previous two years they had also taken part in it, mixing with the children and being adult children themselves. This time there wasn't even the rain to bother them, even if the temperature was cold.

"How much you have grown, young men!" Nigel exclaimed as he saw the children break away from their mum and dad to run towards him and Judith. They threw themselves into their arms and began to shower them with kisses.

"You would make two perfect parents," Tatiana pointed out with a smile. "They couldn't wait to meet you. Thomas also expects you to carry him on his back, dear Nigel."

"Under orders, Captain!"

"Come on champion, you come with me," said Gareth, lifting David, knowing full well what a drama would have unfolded if he had remained on foot.

"Come on, guys, let's start by finding a place; the parade is about to start," Judith urged.

In fact, the floats were already lined up at Piccadilly Circus, each one with its own cartoon or comic book characters, many of which were too recent to be known by Nigel and Judith, who, having no children, had stuck to those of the eighties. Some wriggled on a fire engine, some on a flower-decorated bus, some on the red double-decker bus, some on wagons depicting old yellow train carriages. Bandsmen and majorettes were preparing to leave, moving and hopping in the low temperature not too suitable for the red cloth uniforms of the former and the short white skirts of the latter. Nigel and Gareth, with the children on their shoulders, and Judith and Tatiana fought their way through the crowds along the barriers of Regent Street. The waving of the flags distributed by the organising staff and the shouting of the crowd made the street, decorated with Christmas decorations, even more cheerful. Suddenly, a trumpet call started the parade. Trumpets, timpani and drums in unison began to play a march, punctuated by the footsteps and movements of the majorettes. Behind came the floats, with their characters throwing streamers and confetti at the spectators.

In the riot of colour and music, the children's joy became explosive. They were screaming and waving their arms trying to touch their favourite characters. And for their part, many Batmans and Peppa Pigs reached out towards the crowd, blowing kisses to the crowd.

That whirlwind of fantasy, of uproar and joy, seized the adults almost more than the children. For the children, it was part of their everyday world, albeit in a more fantastic way than usual. For adults, however, it represented a journey back to childhood and to feelings no longer experienced, abandoned and forgotten as the days of maturity had progressed. It was difficult to remain strangers amidst it. No one wanted to stop believing that a superhero could defeat all the villains on earth; or that a blue fairy could change a dress into a very elegant costume, with a touch of a wand, without the disproportionate costs of the great fashion houses; or that in the forests and oceans, animals and plants could sing and dance.

What a wonderful refuge our childhood world provides, Nigel thought. When the cart with the characters from *Mary*

Poppins passed him, he felt that he was a child once again, fascinated by the sweet governess capable of transforming life into a wonderful magical world in which the most beautiful feelings flourished. He told himself that maybe this is what is needed to slow down the tension, fear and poverty of everyday life. Maybe sometimes there's really a need to detach from reality in order to find the most beautiful things that life can offer.

"Uncle Nigel, look! *The Fantastic Four*!"

"Yes, Thomas! Can you see them? Wait, I'll lift you up a little more."

It was Nigel who had passed the love for *The Fantastic Four* to Thomas. According to Nigel, the 'Four' had two crucial elements, compared to the other heroes of his era: a beautiful and intelligent woman who managed to harmonise the group, and a character who was 'different' – without human features – to the point of being called 'the Thing'. Nigel had an entire collection of *Fantastic Four* comics, and every time he went to Gareth and Tatiana's house, he took some to read to his godson, who became equally passionate about them, with an interest incomparable to the way he felt about the newest comic book characters.

"Look, look! *The little Mermaid*! And what are those?" Thomas was pointing to some masks in the shape of flowers.

"Don't you recognise them, love?" Tatiana asked. "Maybe they're characters from some cartoon we haven't seen yet."

"There are so many that they can't even remember them anymore," Gareth whispered, with a small smile, while on his shoulders, David was totally enraptured by the images, colours and music. It was his first toy parade, and his big blue eyes were filled with that enchanted world. The previous year, the rigid temperature had discouraged parents from bringing a child who had just turned one year old.

The band alternated the theme songs of the main cartoons of recent years with the best known and most traditional Christmas songs, those which accompany the television and radio advertisements for panettone and sparkling wine or are broadcast continuously in the big stores from the end of November.

How many times had Nigel, as a child, got lost in those department stores among entire floors filled with Christmas games and childhood dreams, from cars to space shuttles, from a miniature motorcycle to a Lego village, from the model with the little train that circulated in the middle of the mountain houses to the musical drums that so worried the parents! If heaven could mean anything to children, it had come down to Earth in those spaces and, of course, in the candy and ice cream departments, his favourites.

Even today he kept a bag of gummy bears in his office drawer which, especially on long afternoons when he couldn't come up with ideas for his radio show, he swallowed, one after the other.

"Hey, guys, how about we go take refuge in a café soon? It's starting to get a little cold," said Gareth.

"No, Dad! Wait!" Thomas and David replied in unison.

"But wouldn't you like a nice hot chocolate with a mountain of cream on top and coloured marshmallows that sink into it?" This enticement strategy was also unsuccessful.

"Take away the children's toys, take away their world," said Judith smiling.

"Okay, but you take away the heat from me and I sink into the cold!" Gareth complained.

"Oh, come on, don't tell me you're cold!" exclaimed Nigel. "Are you so aged?"

"My friend, I no longer count the white hairs I have."

"But did you know that men with white hair acquire a certain charm?" Judith answered him slyly.

"I always tell him that too," said Tatiana. "And he replies: 'Wife, you don't know what you're saying.' But yes, I know! You men can afford to put on a belly and grow white hair, but when something like this happens to women, your comments are mercilessly negative, like: 'Look how neglected she is; look how she has aged, poor woman! It was once a flower and look how it has shrunk!' Ah, men! Ah, society! It's absurd; we women, complete with our feminism, are still slaves to the pursuit of aesthetic perfection and having to appear at our best!"

"Gareth, how long has it been since you paid your wife a compliment?" said Nigel.

"Nigel, don't be an idiot," Judith scolded. "I think exactly like Tatiana. Watch the ads about women. Spot for not having wrinkles, for dyeing your hair, for being perfumed, for pills for when you're in menopause, for fluid retention, for losing weight... heavens! At most, for you men, advertising is about an amazing car, a symbol of power and success, or coffee, or liqueur. Nothing is asked of you."

"Hey, what's gotten into you? If I had thought that my proposal for a chocolate would have generated the suffragette revolt, I would have remained silent and frozen!" Gareth was still determined.

"You're right," said Tatiana smiling, "the cold is starting to make itself felt. Children, that's enough. Let's go have a snack."

"Yes, the fashion show is ending anyway, you see?" Judith reinforced.

This time Thomas and David seemed more obliging and, aside from small huffs, put up little resistance.

People were beginning to move away from the barriers and

to get back on their way, some among the shops, some instead looking for a place to sit down and warm up.

"I'd say let's go to the Café Royal, shall we?" Nigel offered.

"YES!!!" shouted Thomas who had already forgotten the toy parade and was looking forward to the famous hot chocolate covered with cream and marshmallows.

The place was full, and they managed to find a table only by a miracle. Inside, the red of the warm and welcoming furnishings was combined with that of the Christmas decorations: the balls of the Christmas tree were red, the lollipops hanging from the branches were red and gold, as were the candles on the tables.

The sweets displayed in the window tempted both children and adults. Here were multi-layered cakes interspersed with all kinds of creams and covered with coloured icing, dark chocolate or Chantilly cream, decorated with fruit and almond paste flowers. Among all, one stood out. Four layers filled with dark chocolate cream and covered with cream, with a Santa Claus and small sugar reindeer on top. Next to the cakes were brownies and fairy cakes in dark or milk chocolate, with blueberry or hazelnut creams.

"If I were born again, I would like to be a pastry chef. These desserts are wonderful!" Gareth exclaimed.

"Sure, and your belly would grow even more!" his wife teased him.

The children didn't know whether to stop and look at the sweets or go and admire the Christmas tree. Their mother called them, and they sat down, Thomas on Nigel's lap and David on his father's, just in time to give the orders to the waiter.

In the room, although it was so crowded, the excitement of the street outside remained, and the conversations at the tables flowed calmly.

"I've always loved Christmas!" Judith exclaimed. "For a moment we can really immerse our lives in an atmosphere of happiness and joy."

"It's true, even if our problems remain, we experience them with a different approach and feelings," added Tatiana.

"Who knows, maybe that's because we don't have big problems," Gareth stated, much more cynically.

"Oh, Gareth," Judith said, "every problem is a problem. It depends on who lives it and how they live it. You can't generalise; it's a subjective matter. A child's problems are as important as those of adults, and there is no ranking of more or less serious problems."

"Well, you'll want to admit there's a difference between having cancer and having a broken-down car," Gareth replied.

"Of course, but you can't intervene in the feelings of a person, or in how he perceives and experiences his problems. It may also be that the seriously ill person can find the strength to react to his problems more easily than someone with a broken-down car," Judith replied.

"Perhaps you're right," Tatiana went on, "but it's also true that reducing my problems and thinking that there really are others that are far more serious, helps me to react and not get discouraged. I try to teach my children that we have to be thankful for what we have and that, if something doesn't go well, we shouldn't complain, because this is life and because everyone has problems."

"Okay," replied her friend, "but that doesn't mean we minimise our concerns that the rest of the universe is worse off, because millions of people are hungry and thirsty, or because millions of people are unemployed, or because there are cancer patients or millions of homeless."

"Do you have feelings of guilt?" Gareth asked her sarcastically, causing her friend to frown in surprise.

"Judith, yours – excuse me for telling you – is the typical argument of someone who can't make peace with herself between what she would like to do for others and the world that is falling apart, between the drama of the many and your living in full wellbeing."

Gareth continued, "Give yourself a break. Your problems are important, and no one denies it. But now you can stay warm and drink chocolate. And after a nice walk and a few purchases in some fashion shops on Regent Street, you will return to a warm and comfortable apartment. Tomorrow you will go to work, and at the end of the month, you will have a salary that will allow you to pay the bills. You're not sick, and you're happy with one of the most desired bachelors that I know of. Life smiles at you. If you have a problem tomorrow, it's only right that you worry and despair. And we will suffer with you. But your problem will still be that of a wealthy, young woman. Does this make you feel guilty? You're wrong! That's life. If you weren't there, in your place there would be others."

There was no argument in Gareth's words, only conviction. On the other hand, he was a famous realist. And Nigel who didn't say a word on that occasion, liked it very much.

The arrival of the waiter with six steaming chocolates covered in cream interrupted the discussion for a moment giving way to expressions of amazement: "Wow, this chocolate is truly a triple meal! Until tomorrow morning I can consider myself all right!" Tatiana commented.

"Not bad at all," echoed her husband.

The children immediately dipped the pink and white marshmallows in their drinks, causing the chocolate to overflow from the cup.

"Wait, try not to make too much of a mess!" their mother cried. But they already had half-black chocolate and half-white cream slices.

Laughing, the four adults changed the subject and returned to talking about Christmas and their plans for the day.

When they said goodbye, Nigel and Judith walked towards the National Gallery, in a flood of people that made it difficult to stroll quietly. And Judith asked Nigel the question he expected: "Why didn't you intervene when I argued with Gareth and Tatiana?"

"I didn't think I needed to!"

"I would have liked to know your opinion."

"My opinion? Judith, I have a hard time understanding my opinion too. Certainly, these days I am reflecting on many things, on what we have and on what we continue to demand despite what we have."

"Do you know I've never heard you talk like this?"

"I've never heard myself like this either."

Agbogbloshie, November 27

They were all ready. Their soccer field was a rectangle of packed earth drawn with strips of white lime, four wooden sticks with pieces of cloth at the corners, and between the short sides, two structures, each with three sturdier poles, two uprights joined by a horizontal, to mark the space where it was important to pass the ball or prevent it from passing. And everyone, absolutely everyone, in the whole world would have considered someone who didn't know why the lateral and background white lines were defined in that way – dividing the field in two and crossing a circle – why the lines that marked the spaces were important, why it was called the 'penalty area', who didn't know what the corner flags and goals were, even if the latter lacked the goals intended to collect the ball, in that exciting moment called a goal or just a goal, to be an alien.

Father Angelo's boys all wore different shirts. Sometimes the shirts came from Italy, gifts from old parishioners from a time when his life was different – even if his heart was the same – when he still had black hair. Kofi wore Father Angelo's red Bayern shirt, with his name written in a circle over his heart topped with stars.

Father Angelo gave them to the others on important occasions, and each time he explained that they were from Italian teams. Two more were also red, but with yellow collars and cuffs. Some were blue with four stripes running across the chest, two white above and below, one red and one black, and a strange design also on the heart. Father Angelo had said it represented a sailor with a pipe, but the boys knew the sailors and fishermen of the Korle Lagoon and they didn't look like that drawing. Still other shirts were half red and half blue with a drawing of a strange animal. Father Angelo called it a griffin. Then there was the one that Father Angelo never assigned. He called it the 'jersey of glory'.

The boys of the opposing team, on the other hand, had shirts which were all the same, with horizontal green and white stripes. They had come from Dzorwulu, a neighbourhood of Accra, pretentiously defined as residential but also full of poor people's shacks. Among these worked Father Ethan, local head of the missionary family to which Father Angelo also belonged. Father Ethan, co-organiser of the match, was a Scotsman, and it was said that the green and white striped shirts were his own and were those of his favourite team.

Everything was ready for the match – a real and important match. Even if the players were all barefoot, soccer shoes, the kind with studs so as not to slip, would have been unthinkable for children who often didn't have shoes of any kind. The teams were Korle's Antelopes, the home team, and Dzorwulu's Warthogs. None of the boys had actually ever seen an antelope or a warthog, but they were the names that populated the stories told by their fathers and grandfathers, the stories of their families' homelands before the capital swallowed them up, the stories of the hundred Ghanaian ethnic groups who in the big city on the ocean were looking for a way to be a single people.

While the boys were getting ready for the match, the public happily lined up on the sides of the pitch; on one side the people of Agbogbloshie, on the other the people of Dzorwulu. At the end they would mix for a great collective lunch, prepared together by the nuns and all the mothers.

That day there were also men, all football experts and ardent fans, ready to incite, to contest, to yell at the twenty-two players. There were also some teachers who had worked their hard apprenticeships in Father Angelo's school. And there were even two French journalists, who had come to report on life in this place forgotten by the world, who had learned of the meeting and were ready to write about the 'football match in the trash'.

Father Angelo didn't like this joyful rendezvous becoming the subject of a journalistic denunciation and he had insisted that the two not speak to the children.

"Are you sure of this, Father Angelo?" one of the two journalists had said maliciously. "In our opinion, the boys would be happy if we talked about them!"

"What are you looking for?" said Father Angelo. "Even in professional football, you need to ask the clubs' permission to interview players. And for children in your home, you would have a parental release. And I don't think you thought of bringing the forms with you." Then his voice had hardened: "My concern or not, I'll make you regret coming here if you don't respect these conditions. In these places, offenders risk paying dearly."

"Don't get too excited, Father, and remember that you are a priest of Santa Romana Church. Some allusions aren't good for you," said the journalist.

The priest understood that he had been wrong, if not on the merits of the matter, certainly in the tone and words he had used. But then he acquitted himself. He had invented that soccer tournament and would never allow anyone to distort the spirit with which it was born.

The Korle Antelopes were already in formation for the traditional photograph before the game started. Father Angelo thought that photographs told people's lives and stories better than any words, and as soon as he could, he gathered the images of the children into a big book available to everyone, in what he called a bit pompously the 'canonical'.

Here were photos taken while they were at school, while they attended Christian and other church services, while they played football, while singing.

And there were also pictures of the adults in the village. There were two of Abenà, one while she was working with the sewing machine at the Centro where she earned some money as a seamstress, the other with her husband, who once came to pick her up on his way back from his day's fishing. There was a photo of Mama Bon outside her grocery store, with a crate of pineapples next to her, those green pineapples that look unripe to Westerners but in fact, have a very sweet white pulp, when fully ripe.

There was a photo of Marc, the carpenter who had repeatedly arranged and adjusted the poor furniture of the Centre as well as the doors and flags in the corner of the soccer field. Small moments of that life were always punctuated by the same actions and the same rhythms: a life between work, children, hardships and illnesses.

Still, the faces in those photos were smiling. And the eleven boys posing smiled.

"Why are there eleven players?" Ama had asked him this one day, and he had come up with a joke that the little girl certainly hadn't understood: "Because that way there isn't the one who betrays."

Kofi stood in the centre of the group, his expression proud, and his chest thrust out to show his Bayern shirt, with a white cloth band knotted around his left arm, because he was the captain of the Antelopes. And he felt his mother's proud gaze upon him. He wished her face always looked so joyful. He would have liked a magic brush to erase every wrinkle, every sign left by the hours and hours of work at the sewing machine and at home while she was cooking and washing. This was his mum, the most beautiful woman in the world, and he wanted to give her the whole world. And that day he promised to give and dedicate at least one goal to her. Then Father Angelo whistled for the start of the game, amidst a cacophony of shouts, applause and chants for one or the other team.

They were children, ignorant of tactics and schemes, in spite of the advice of those fathers who from time to time appoint themselves amateur coaches. But they were two teams, made cohesive by the mutual knowledge and friendship they had always had. And football was in their blood. None of them would probably ever participate in a winning world championship, probably none of them would have reached professional status with its million-dollar lifestyle. But it was a pleasure to watch them.

Father Angelo would have preferred to enjoy the match among the spectators instead of having to concentrate attention on his task as referee. For him, a great Napoli fan, with a love that neither his years in Genoa nor those in Africa had affected, the passion for football was as alive as that for books and music, a still strong bond with the world where he was born and lived. And the few times he found a way to go to the mission's headquarters in Accra, where there was practically always electricity and there was also a satellite television with a channel dedicated to European football, he came back a happy child. Sometimes they even broadcast Napoli matches live.

This was the strong legacy of his past life, when with his

friends, and decked out in a scarf in the colours of his team, he had spent Sunday afternoons at the stadium. He continued to know all the Napoli players and all the formations of the last twenty years by heart. He had played himself, for a few years, for a small club in his city, and he showed promise. Then, as often happens, a different path had opened up for him. His had been the priesthood. Once he understood how essential it was for him, it didn't take him long to make a decision that revolutionised his life, and from which he would never go back. He always said that each person has to choose at a certain point, and the important thing is to take a stand without regrets.

When he arrived in Africa, he certainly could not suppress his passion, and among 'his' children, he had found fertile ground to cultivate it. Here, one could not speak of the 'opium of the masses' as they increasingly did in the West. But now, the ninety minutes of a match allowed him to catch his breath and take a step away from the problems and anxieties of a tiring and all-engulfing everyday life.

Soccer and music acted as a bridge between his present life in Agbogbloshie, where he had formed new friendships and developed a bond with the local impoverished community, and his past, first in Naples and then in Genoa. Of course, his missionary centre on the edge of the landfill was very different from the parish where he had lived and served for years in the small inlet of Boccadasse in Genoa, in the church of San Francesco overlooking the sea.

There was no regret, only sweetness and gratitude for the gifts received, as he thought every day about his rock at Boccadasse, where early in the morning, in summer and winter, he went for coffee with his fishermen friends in the small boat shed, and where in a corner there was a small kitchenette with a coffee machine. Beside the infinite expanse of that sea, shaded in the different blues of the sky, he met them in the morning when they returned from fishing and in the evening before they went back to sea, to talk about everything and nothing, from politics to health, to cooking, to the family. And sometimes of God.

Father Angelo had become one of them, to the point that for those fishermen it was not infrequent to forget his habit and make trivial jokes even in his presence. And if he didn't like their jokes much, this contributed to making him feel totally included in that small group of sea-loving people. Of course, the lives of the sailor and the fisherman are difficult and poor at every latitude.

But here, in Agbogbloshie, there was not even the blue of the Mediterranean. On the shore of the lagoon, facing the ocean, it hurt him that water near the coast was made dark by the river that poured its poisons into it. Kofi's father had told him that before returning from fishing on his boat, despite the extra weight, they took on board two large tanks of water collected off the coast, where it was still clear, which served to get rid of the splashes of that last stretch of the black waves that the boat had to ride by force of oars in order to reach land. And it was no coincidence that that man and many others like him allowed themselves, as the only, very rare luxury on important occasions, to visit one of the paid freshwater showers along the way to the Port of Tema.

No, there was no longer anything that could remind Father Angelo of Boccadasse, in the natural port near which the capital of Ghana had developed over the centuries. And he missed the historic centre of Genoa, so large and so enclosed within itself; he missed Via del Campo, with the shop that exclusively sold the records of his favourite singer, Fabrizio De André, whose song *Volta la Carta* he had taught to his Agbogbloshie babies, certain that one day they would give it the meaning that he had found in it, of the eternal turn of things, of the belief that fate doesn't necessarily have to remain nailed to a landfill. And he missed the *carruggi,* the narrow streets in the heart of the historic centre, where amidst the smells of multi-ethnic food and shops and clubs of all kinds, humanity of different origins and profiles moved: students, prostitutes, transvestites, migrants, tourists, citizens. He had spent many of his days there in contact with those people who, perhaps more than others, might need his word or his help, a piece of bread or a place to stay. In Genoa, as in many other places in Italy, there were shacks and dumps, populated by people exhausted by poverty and lack of hope.

But then the time had come for Father Angelo to go among those who were even more needy. In the five years he had spent in Agbogbloshie, he had discovered how true another verse of De André's song was. He had understood the common sign between his new family and that of Genoa. Among the waste and hunger of the African landfill, as well as among the poverty and vice of the most hidden streets of the Ligurian city, people who smelled good were born and grew like flowers.

London, December 9

"How is your programme coming along, Nigel? Two days left," the manager said, in his hoarse voice.

"I'm collecting information and documents. It will be ready by the 11th," Nigel answered.

"I remind you that it is a report of five minutes at the most on the garbage of our city. So get on with it. You don't have to win a Pulitzer."

"I'm certain. Keep calm."

"Keep calm? The last time they told me that was when I was getting married. And the effects have been devastating."

The line was abruptly cut off by the handset of the telephone being lowered. Mike embodied the perfect director, surly and synthetic, with not a word more than necessary.

An envelope had recently arrived on Nigel's desk, with one word, "Agbogbloshie" written on it. Nigel opened it, and inside he found a stack of typed, collated papers, with drawings of curves and hyperbolas, and index cards detailing metallic and gaseous substances. The first page had the title: *"Results of medical analyses on samples. Children of Agbogbloshie."* Above was a message from Kurt:

"Dear Nigel, in addition to what I have already given you, I am also sending you the medical report drawn up by our contact person who has just returned. This is medical research data, very technical and perhaps of little impact for your radio audience. However, it may be useful to you. I think it is appropriate that you

meet this expert before your programme."

Kurt was right about the use of technicalities in his broadcast. A programme like this couldn't contain medical terms that would be incomprehensible to non-experts, and which would certainly have had a soporific effect within a few seconds. He would have to try to draw out the essence of those results, and surely, meeting the doctor who had drafted it would be useful.

For Nigel, this programme was a risk. Changing Mike's brief, to criticise the garbage collection system in the city, certainly gave him more breathing space. But that did not guarantee listeners would have an equal interest in a political denunciation of the administrative dysfunctions that most directly concerned them.

"It's still a very important report, Nigel." Judith comforted him at lunchtime, over a sandwich and a bottle of beer, in the park below the radio headquarters. "You're taking the right approach to the subject you have to deal with."

"Hopefully, Judith. I hope Mike thinks so too."

"Oh, Nigel, the world is globalised now. What happens on the streets here is connected to what happens elsewhere. And a theme of this depth can only find ample breadth. What did Mike want?" said Judith.

"Could I just point the finger at such-and-such alderman or such-and-such head of municipal services," Nigel said. "But my programme could have a much stronger political impact than that."

"In what way?" Judith asked.

"Imagine that Mike, for whatever reason I don't know, wanted to attack this administration. That's when the programme he asked me to make would meet his expectations. If, instead, I talk about how Africa's discharges are fed by the western world,

I'm going to hit a topic that is certainly very interesting but has little in common with the interests of our much smaller and more banal city."

"I see," Judith agreed, biting into her tomato salad and light cheese sandwich.

Her choice of lunch was always rather different from Nigel's beefier frankfurter mustard sandwich. Whenever they decided to have lunch together in the park – not always possible due to both of their jobs – they went to a little shop under Nigel's office that made all kinds of toast and sandwiches, with all different shapes and compositions of bread. After at least two years, the managers knew them and enjoyed their contrasting attentions to 'light' and 'fat' respectively. For Judith, the best thing was to stuff the sandwich with a little 'strictly light' cream cheese, otherwise only tomatoes, vegetables or shrimps. For Nigel, on the other hand, if he wanted to be 'light', he chose a turkey burger with mustard. Otherwise, it was frankfurters and fries, seasoned with mayonnaise.

"However," Judith continued, "it seems to me that you have come up with an interesting idea which is very rarely talked about. I hope you can take your programme in this direction. But you'll have to prepare Mike. When will you tell him?"

"Actually, I think I won't tell him. In fact, I'm not deviating from the theme he gave me. I've just given him a different perspective, exercising my freedom as a journalist."

"You're probably right. But be prepared in case you don't like what happens."

Nigel had always appreciated Judith's gentle, delicate way of telling someone what they should do, without ever intervening assertively. He thought it a rare quality in a world of people who compete to teach their fellows something.

"Don't doubt it; I am. There's just one aspect that I don't understand in this whole affair. I confess that I am very taken by it, but I still lack something to 'feel' the programme, to make it… how to say this… mine. There is still a gap that I can't fill."

"I don't think you need to be completely engaged by every programme you make, Nigel. You wouldn't have much a life if you are."

"Sure, but this is different. It touched me in a particular way, perhaps because it is my first programme with a social aspect. What I'm reading in the reports Kurt gave me, and everything he and Joel told me, stays with me all the time. I finish my music programme in the morning, and I immediately start thinking about how to make what I will tell my listeners on the 11th true, really true and sincere. But I still can't find the formula, the key to open the closed doors that I still have inside me, to let in those people who live and die of our waste."

"Maybe you never will, Nigel. Maybe you need to see people's faces for their story to become yours. When you talk about music, that world belongs to you; you talk about yourself, what you have experienced since you were a child, your childhood, your parents, your youth, your generation, in short, your world. You only know about the landfill in Africa because Kurt and Joel told you about it or because you read about it. You may be disgusted by it, but in some part of your mind, you know it doesn't belong to you that much, because you don't live among garbage and open sewers, and you don't see people scrambling through poverty and children playing on piles of garbage."

Judith was right, he could never have made that reality his own until he had mixed among those people. But that didn't prevent him from trying.

Agbogbloshie, November 27

The Antelopes and the Warthogs moved quickly on the football field. The match was intense and basically fair. Father Angelo's whistle was hardly heard, and certainly less than the screams of the public and the coaches, real or presumed.

One official supporter of the Antelopes was Nii's father, who was considered a character among the children's community. He was the cook assigned to international breakfasts in a large hotel in Accra. Whenever he could, he brought home something the customers hadn't consumed: pancakes, eggs, toast, even little jars with some jam left over in them. His children, and others who sometimes enjoyed the treats, were especially crazy about pancakes. For this occasion, the day before, he had procured enough for all the little athletes of both teams, and it would be his prize for everyone at the end of the game.

He loved football as much, and perhaps more, than Father Angelo. As a boy, he had played well and was said to have narrowly missed the call-up for the Under-17's in Italy. The name he had chosen for his own son was that of Nii Lamptey, the outstanding player of that national team of champion boys. Nii's father had a day off every week and had gladly accepted Father Angelo's request to take care of the team, above all to share a common passion with his son. Now, like his counterpart on the Warthog team, he scurried along the sidelines of the field, shouting directions to the boys. But even if they had wanted to listen, they would not have been able to. The voices of the two men were lost in the shouts and choruses of the spectators.

Father Angelo had repeated to everyone that the important thing was just to play and have fun, that participating counted more than winning. But the children knew nothing of Pierre de Coubertin and his ideas. And perhaps in that respect, Father Angelo was not convinced enough and therefore not convincing.

No, the Antelopes and the Warthogs wanted to win. They wanted to get on the wooden bench that at the end of the game, the cleric would raise as the podium for the winners, while the losers would line up next to them but with their feet on the ground. Every player would have a wooden and rope necklace, but for the winners, the carpenter Marc had prepared eleven wooden medals engraved with the word 'Winner'.

After twenty minutes, Kofi scored his goal to dedicate to his mother, and to make it clear to everyone, he escaped the embrace of his teammates and ran to the sidelines to embrace her. However, shortly afterwards the Warthogs drew level and so it was time for halftime.

In the second half, it was Nii who scored the winning goal, and his father and coach were the first to embrace him. At the end of the game, the people of Agbogbloshie invaded the field in jubilation, and this time Ama was the fastest, faster than Mum and Dad, running to hug her brother.

It was just a football match, but in that moment, that field had become the centre of their whole world. Father Angelo, also satisfied and joyful, had begun to photograph all the little football players with their parents and friends, from both teams, now confused with each other. There is the moment of competition and the moment of sharing – that was the moment to experience the joy of being together. The rest was deferred to the next game.

For the awards ceremony, the entire audience lined up in

order around the field, as silent as it had been that day. The Antelopes and the Warthogs lined up in two rows, and all the respective players were called by name by Father Angelo, with a megaphone, to receive their necklaces. First the defeated and then the victors who hoisted themselves proudly onto the wooden bench. Father Angelo drove out his uneasiness, in feeling that maybe his children would never have more important prizes in their life.

Father Ethan felt the same lump in his throat, thinking that many of these children, despite the efforts of the mission, would never hear their names called at any high school graduation party. But then happiness prevailed, because if there is suffering in life, it is not everything. And, as always in Africa, sharing food was a celebration and joy for everyone, and nothing that was needed was missing: the meat jollof rice, very similar to the Spanish paella, the *kyemgbu* crabs but with cassava paste, the fried plantain germ *kelewele* spiced with ginger, the beer for the adults who could drink it, for the others and for the children, the *askenkee,* the fresh, white drink made with wheat that even Father Angelo liked much more than he had ever liked barley water.

At a certain point during lunch, the Antelope players, accompanied by Ama and little Osagyefo, reached Father Angelo who was going around the different groups, greeting the adults who stopped him to thank him and congratulate him on the organisation.

"My boys! You did great."

"Thank you, Father," they chorused, but it was clear they weren't there to be praised.

"What is it, guys?"

"Do you have an extra necklace?"

"No, but you know, there is a precise number for the players."

"Yes, but one is missing and has been replaced today."

Father Angelo jumped and turned his face away from the children so fragile and with their eyes so big, for fear of showing emotion. How had he not thought about it?

"You're right, for Aziz there is a different but equally important award. Wait for me here." He ran inside the Centre, and shortly afterwards, came out with a small package from which a flap of blue fabric was sticking out. "Let's go."

When they entered Aziz's house, they found him in bed waiting for the broth that his mother was preparing for him. The boy got up.

"How did it go, guys?"

"We won. We tore them up!" replied Osagyefo. "Kofi and Nii scored two legendary goals that knocked them all down."

"Wow!"

"And if you had been there, we would have done the third one too, you know? You must recover soon. We are not the same without you," Kwame prompted.

"Thanks, thanks, guys. I was hoping you'd come and tell me how it went, and I was hoping you'd won."

"We won! Look, you're still part of our team," Martin said.

"Thank you. This little award is really beautiful, you know."

"It is true. But that's not the only award. We had a team award, and we want you to have it," Kofi said.

Aziz looked at them curiously, but the most amazed was Father Angelo. He had said nothing to the boys, and they had not only understood what the prize was as soon as they saw the package but had also known how to offer it to Aziz better than he could ever have done himself. He began to unwrap the gift. There was the Napoli shirt with number 10, Maradona's shirt, the greatest ever. Ama helped Father Angelo remove the paper and placed the shirt on Aziz's chest.

"They all want you to keep it."

"But... Father Angelo... this is the shirt of glory! What do I have to do with it?" asked Aziz.

"You have something to do with it; this shirt belongs to all of you, to a team of champions. And you have to start wearing it yourself," explained the priest.

"But I didn't play!" the boy scoffed.

"Not today, but you're on the team. We want you to keep it," reiterated his companions.

"Guys, now that the team's complete, how about a nice photo?" Father Angelo proposed, determined to overcome his emotion and satisfied with having kept the camera around his neck.

"Yes, okay!"

The quickest to get on the bed and embrace Aziz was little Osagyefo, careful however not to cover the shirt of glory on his friend's chest.

London, December 9

"Hi, Kurt. I need to talk to you." Nigel called as soon as he got back to the office after lunch with Judith in the park.

"Have you received everything?"

"Yes, yes. But I need to talk to you. Can we meet for a moment at the Café Noir?"

"Okay, but not for a couple of hours."

"All right. Later."

The same pretty waitress from three days ago came to take the orders.

"Prosecco?" Kurt asked.

Nigel looked at him curiously. He would have thought him the type for stronger drinks. "Me too," he repeated almost without thinking.

Kurt seemed to read his mind:

"A few years ago, I almost killed a woman with her baby. After work I had been drinking with some friends. I didn't think I was drunk, but I probably drank too much. In fact, let's say I was drunk. I took the car and headed home. I hit a woman with a child she was holding by the hand, and both ended up in hospital. The mother left after three days with simple bruises; the son remained in intensive care for a week. Every day I stood there outside his room and prayed. Luckily, the little one recovered. When the situation was over, I promised myself I would never take hard liquor again; at most I would drink one glass of wine a day, no more, and only when I knew I wasn't going to use the car.

This is my glass of wine today."

"I'm honoured that you decided to consume it with me, then."

"Let's get to the point, Nigel," Kurt said after this brief moment of confession.

"The point is, I've read the whole report; I've seen all the photos you sent me. It's all extremely clear, poignant and interesting. All this will be of great use to me for the programme."

"But...?"

"But I need something more. I need to feel it's mine like all the other programmes I've done. You see, Kurt, when you talk on the radio, people only hear your voice. They don't see your face; they don't see your eyes. In those five minutes, your voice must be able to capture the world. And I don't capture it if what I say I don't feel."

"Nigel, what you claim is impossible. Do you want to experience something you discovered just a few days ago as a part of you? It's not only impossible, it is... incorrect."

"Incorrect? What do you mean?"

"In your thirst to make that distant world your own, there is all the arrogance and presumption of wanting to know, understand and resolve realities that only by living like those miserable people over there, in that land forgotten by all, is it possible to know understand and solve. We live in our comfortable apartments, and we don't even know what it means to have a kitchen, bathroom and bed in eight square metres. We don't know the nauseating smell of these hovels, surrounded by rubbish, rats, cockroaches and open-air sewers. And what do we do? We send the officials of the big international institutions to do the usual annual report, some pseudo-activist or some celebrity to be filmed with the children and with the women...

which always has a great effect, of course. Too bad that the same champions of justice then travel first class, stay in luxury hotels, and live in mega suites of three hundred square meters in Manhattan. And the paradox is that these same people come to teach what must be done against poverty and against environmental disasters. Light years away from these problems, which they themselves have helped to generate.

"Loving the good life in our homes, changing into a different outfit every day, driving luxury cars is all just taking away from the many to give to the few... those same few who then go to take pictures with the children of the refugee camps or who come to speak at conferences on how we should live and what we should do to save the world. Don't tell me now that you have to feel it's yours. Do you really want to feel it's yours? Go and live with those poor souls, and you will truly feel it as yours."

As Kurt spoke, his deep black eyes looked straight at Nigel and his voice weighed up every word. His was anger and sadness. But there was no resignation, only awareness.

"Don't you think you're being too stiff, Kurt?" said Nigel. "Maybe what you say is true, but you can't blame those who are well just because others are sick."

"No, Nigel, in fact, I'm not blaming anyone. I'm just telling you the arrogant falsehood that revolves around this world. There are many people who have to thank the dramas of others for their parliamentary seats, and their fame, which they have been able to exploit. Just as there are many former politicians who, no longer having a seat in the House or a need to arrange some children without art or part, recycle themselves with pseudo-cooperatives or non-profit organisations for the protection of fundamental rights or for development cooperation. Unfortunately, there is very often a family and patronage management in financing projects for the development and strengthening of rights that has nothing to do with the goals for which they are set, going instead to line only the pockets of some sad bureaucrat or of his family."

"Kurt, what you're saying is very harsh. I personally know many activists, aid workers and freelancers who sincerely work in international aid and cooperation. And I know their souls and their minds are honest, and they don't work for others just to get rich or further their careers."

"I do not deny that there are those who sincerely do it. And I think I'm one of them. But there are many who work in international projects and cooperation just for the money or to make a name for themselves. They go there, among the poorest and most desperate, they pretend to be interested in them and have a few photos taken together which then go into all the tabloids. They then use European or international funding to set up little projects, and then they go back, in first class, to their homes and to sleep in five-star hotels or penthouses with swimming pools and built-in spas.

"I'm not saying they shouldn't have all this, if they have worked hard and earned and deserved it. But at least let these first-class people not be presented to us as champions of the causes of the most miserable! If they want to do charity work, let them do it without advertising it. If they want to go to Africa to help, let them do so without being photographed with intense and sorrowful faces next to starving children. If they want to defend the victims of war and international crimes, let them do so without letting them talk about the clothes they change every day or the villas they live in. And, at least, be sure the money goes to those who carry out real projects that are actually useful to the beneficiaries. Do you also understand that there is huge hypocrisy here?"

"Of course I understand. And I also understand that, if you talk about it, it's because you lived it. But do you have specific names for these accusations of yours?"

"I have enough experience to be sure, rather than relying on perception, even if not based on evidence. For the rest, just open any gossip magazine that advertises the latest 'missionary' journey of some VIP. It's not an absolute bad thing; don't get me wrong. All right, it allows us to at least talk about what is happening in the world. But I don't think the battles against poverty and crimes against humanity can be fought by people with lifestyles that are opposite to the problems they think they can solve and for which, perhaps, they may partially be responsible – even though the small and miserable life of each of us can hardly be the cause of the world's problems."

While Nigel reflected on what he was listening to, Kurt continued like a flooded river:

"I would just like more authenticity in the world of cooperation and the protection of fundamental rights. Instead, many create careers or build their characters on the misfortunes of others. This saddens me. And it saddens me even more to think that by now, our world doesn't even notice the falsehoods in which it is immersed. You tell me you want to hear the story of the poor people who are in the dump? But with what pretension do you say this? With what arrogance do you think you can own a life that doesn't belong to you and that is a thousand light years away from you? If you can understand the problem and have a thought for those who live in that dimension, for at least one minute a day of your life for your next few years, you have already reached an enormous milestone. If you then want to make it yours, leave everything and go and live there. But that's another story."

Nigel felt confused, but this time he didn't get offended or irritated. "Kurt, I'm not that insensitive. The need to feel the reality I'm going to talk about as mine was, and is, sincere. I do however realise what you mean. Maybe sometimes we are so caught up in ourselves that we cannot overcome our dimension and our experience, with its riches but also with its limitations.

"That does not, however, prevent us from being interested in what we understand is not right and also from fighting for it to become a little fairer," Kurt added. "Nigel, make your programme and do it in the best way so that the Africans of the Agbogbloshie neighbourhood are the real protagonists. Nobody else. They must be the protagonists. And it is they who will interest people. In those five minutes of time, give them a voice and tell their stories. It's not your voice, so much as theirs, that your listeners need to feel authentic. You cannot and must not expect yourself to live in symbiosis with them. You are a journalist. You've documented yourself and you need to document your listeners, right? I don't think you have to change your identity, but you have to make yourself conscious and involved, the instrument of the pains and joys of those you go to tell." Kurt had taken on an almost paternal tone, so different from the brusque and not always friendly manner he'd had so far. And Nigel was impressed.

"I don't often speak my mind anymore… and maybe this glass of wine helped me too much today," Kurt continued with a half-smile. "You know, Nigel, there comes a time when you don't feel like saying anything anymore. We are tired of repeating the same things, the same speeches in the face of a reality that never seems to change. This is why it is necessary to have people who translate the silence of those who no longer have words, because they are too tired."

"And you, Kurt, do you still have words?"

Kurt's gaze seemed to get lost in that glass of wine. And he didn't answer Nigel's question.

Agbogbloshie, November 28

"If we don't hurry up with the gift, we'll never make it!"

That morning the seven children who were on their way to the sorceress' house – Aziz was missing; still too weak – were more anxious and less sleepy than usual.

"Do you know that we don't even know the sorceress' name?" Ama observed.

They had immediately called her 'sorceress', on seeing her tall and blonde, dressed in white, in that room full of strange instruments whose purpose they didn't understand. No one had thought to ask her what her name was. It was enough for them to immediately understand the kindness of her heart. And then, there were those secret appointments not to be told to anyone, not even to the other children.

"It's true we don't know her real name, but she... is the sorceress," Palletta replied. "And by the way, yes, we have to hurry, otherwise we'll never be able to give her the gift. Father Angelo, are you sure that the sorceress will leave this weekend?"

"Yes, guys, I'm sure."

"Don't worry," Nelson said, "we'll make it. The computer is practically ready; only a few minor repairs are missing."

"Father Angelo," Ama asked, "you're the only white man left with us. Everyone else leaves almost immediately. Why?"

"Why am I staying here, or why aren't the others? Agbogbloshie is the place that I have chosen for me. For others, it is different. People travel, Ama, and it's normal for them to come and then leave."

"Okay, but we in Agbogbloshie have nothing but the landfill. Why then do they come?"

"I don't know, my child."

He knew it very well, but he couldn't tell those children that it was precisely the dump that explained those 'hit and run' visits by so many white people. Journalists and officials from large humanitarian organisations arrived. Everyone showed interest and disdain, and everyone left with the commitment to raise awareness of what was happening in that place. He rarely had the opportunity to hear from anyone again or to see them again. For him, upon his arrival five years earlier in the mission in Accra, it had been normal to choose that place, those people. He was now one of them. He was the only white man not forced to submit to the extortions of petty crime gangs who set up checkpoints along the roads leading to the lagoon, as indeed in many areas of the great suburbs of Accra.

"Love, it's not true that we have nothing!" Kofi insisted vehemently. "We even have a soccer field! Not everyone in the other places has that. And we do."

"It's true, and it's thanks to Father Angelo that he stayed with us for so long," Palletta recalled.

"The field was already there when I arrived," corrected the priest.

"It was not like this. It was just a patch of land," Kofi retorted.

"I'm sorry the sorceress is leaving. She's always been good to us," Osagyefo said.

"I figured even she'd be with us for a long time," Nii added.

"Imagining hurts. Sometimes dreaming is worse than living reality. It can become a dangerous entertainment if the walls that surround living don't open but shrink," Kofi ruled.

The other boys had got used to certain phrases from their companion, but Father Angelo was taken by surprise. He knew his babies would, sooner or later, understand that they were not able to overcome the barriers that prevented their dreams from turning into projects. But it was early, too early to see them disillusioned and to suffer for it. It was too early for Ama to know that no prince of England would ever marry her. Too soon for Nelson to understand that he would never go to Mars to meet David Bowie. Too soon for Kofi to stop hoping to see the Bayern stadium and to understand that all his football would be that of the Antelopes.

This damned dump! Father Angelo screamed to himself. Each of those dreams had been formed from that pile of rubbish, from Ama's magazines to the machine for making sweets, perhaps a gift to some lucky northern child of the world thrown away after a few days of play but for Palletta, Nii and Martin had become a job prospect for adults.

But it was too early for reality, like a terrible storm which would break the fragile branches of trees, sweep away those dreams, hurt their souls, just as the landfill hurt their bodies. He knew his job was to be there for them when the present took them by the throat and they felt denied the future. He had known many men and women, in Italy and in Ghana, who had lost themselves like this, in the bitter disappointment of what they had never had. *But not yet for these little ones, Lord, please.*

Many times, with patience and discretion, he had tried to inculcate in those children the idea that joy is not made of material things, to help them think that serenity and peace can be found anywhere, that every moment life offers them could be a gift of God, to be able to recognise and accept him. "Let the children come to me," Jesus repeated in his heart. *But not like this, Lord, not by this atrocious way; not with this life, please!*

"Kofi is strange these days, Father Angelo. He makes speeches that we don't understand," said Palletta.

"I'm not weird!" protested Kofi. "But do you believe that we can really have what we want? Look at our parents; why should we have a life different from theirs?"

"You see, Kofi," he turned to him, and to all the others, and Father Angelo said, "I have to tell you a thought that I have every time I see a field with flowers. You know those flowers too, right? The flowers, like those big blue lilies that are along the river before the lagoon opens up. Where I come from there are many others of many colours. Sometimes you find yourself in an immense field, endless in our eyes. But it would be nothing if a few flowers didn't grow there. They stand on thin stems and have petals as fragile as a butterfly's wings. Yet they are so strong that they often manage to overcome even the wind and the rain. Their whole life is consumed in what, for us, would be a few days. But as long as they live, they fill that infinite field with colour and perfume, which would not be the same without them. No two are alike even though they may appear to be. I believe that each of us is like those flowers. Everyone has their frailties, their limits, but life on this earth would not be the same if even one of us did not exist."

"Father Angelo, does this mean that we too, all of us in this group, are like flowers?"

"Oh yes, Ama, among the most beautiful and fragrant flowers."

"Well... then we have to decide which flowers we want to be!" Osagyefo said.

"It's obvious, we must be blue lilies; you know them!"

Palletta exclaimed.

"No, we must be the blossoms of the flamboyant tree. Mum always talks about it. They are beautiful, of a bright red colour, and they stand high, higher than the tall grass of the savannah," replied Ama.

"We should be roses, instead," the sure voice of Kofi spoke up.

"Why roses, Kofi?" Nii asked.

"How are they?" Osagyefo asked.

"Remember what Grandpa Baba said? They grow in Kenya, red as blood, and according to him, in other places too. And they are special. When they are small, their petals are all attached to each other as if to enclose and protect something precious. Then they slowly open up to let go. They have a very good smell, better than that of sweets and candies. Then they start to fall, as if the roses were people who get older and lose something with each passing day."

"Father Angelo, have you been to Kenya? Have you ever seen roses?"

"No, I've never been to Kenya, but roses also grow in many other parts of the world, and I've seen them often."

"And they are like Grandfather Baba says? Are they red and flamboyant?"

"Those in Kenya, yes, they are red and, they are called Bourbon roses, but elsewhere they grow white, yellow, pink ones. Indeed, the colour pink takes its name from them. And there are even some with petals which are coloured gold at the bottom and have a sort of red collar higher up."

"Do you have any photographs of them? I'd like to see them," Ama asked.

"But this is better! You can see the roses carved on the statue of the Madonna which is in the Centre."

"Oh! I thought they were invented images."

"No, Osagyefo, those are the roses."

"Then we have them here too. We could be called the Roses of Agbogbloshie!" Kofi suggested confidently.

"I like being like a rose," Ama said.

"Sure, you're a girl and you want a dress that colour. But what do we have to do with it?" Palletta protested.

"But you really are tuna! What does the dress have to do with it?" the little girl yelled at him. But then she realised that her companion was just teasing her a little.

Father Angelo was ready to propose a compromise between the fact that roses are inflected in the feminine but flowers generally in the masculine, but he realised that it was not necessary. Everyone was excited about the name and the idea. Kofi also seemed to return to his less gloomy and more carefree mood when his child's face did not betray adult thoughts. And the Agbogbloshie Roses went to meet the sorceress for the last time.

London, December 10

It was a very cold morning with a grey sky. The traffic in London was exacerbated by the frenzy of the pre-Christmas period. An overflowing crowd came and went from the shops at all hours of the day.

Nigel had an appointment with Kurt's 'expert' at four p.m. in front of the Café Concerto, opposite the Harrods department store. Nigel knew the expert was a doctor who had lived in Agbogbloshie for months. But more than that, he was looking for something, a testimony, a story, that would help him give life to the first programme he had ever made that didn't talk about music.

"Are you sure it's just because it's different from your other programmes?" Judith had asked him that morning, seeing him more and more involved.

Judith's questions were never thrown at random. For the first time, Nigel was beginning to feel responsible for something he hadn't committed to directly and personally, and for which he didn't suffer at least some of the consequences. It wasn't like the much-discussed issue of climate, the greenhouse effect. He knew that he too was contributing to it in some way, but the fact that he too was a victim eased his sense of guilt. This was different. Among the victims of the landfill, he was not there.

He showed up for the appointment on time. It was very cold, and people were walking quickly up and down the street to keep warm. Many expected a snowy Christmas, even if the forecasts had ruled it out. Nigel hoped the forecasters were wrong. He would have preferred a white Christmas, like one he remembered of many years ago on the morning of the 25th when he had gone with his father to the park to play snowballs, while his mother was preparing lunch for them, his grandparents and uncles. That morning, he had played so much with his father, throwing himself in the snow, that once they got home, they had both had to change all their clothes, even their underwear.

A blonde girl with a white wool hat and a large blue and Havana checked scarf over a long grey coat approached him with a quick step.

"Nigel?" she asked confidently.

"Yes, it's me," he answered, a little surprised, actually pleasantly surprised, at the girl's attractiveness.

"Hi, I'm Catherine. Kurt must have told you about me."

"Good morning, Catherine. That's right, Kurt told me that I was going to meet with his contact person, a doctor. May I offer you a coffee?"

"I'd love that."

They entered, and a waiter led them to a free table. "Here's the menu, but we also serve the house Christmas coffee, with chocolate, rum and cream."

"Thanks, a regular coffee for me," said Catherine.

"Me too," Nigel agreed.

At the next table, there were chocolate cakes dipped in cream and the big happy laughter of a small family with two children.

"It's good to see these children so happy, isn't it?" Catherine began.

Nigel smiled nodding.

"I arrived a week ago from Accra, where I lived for five months on the edge of the Agbogbloshie landfill. I did research there on the effects of the material accumulated on the health of the inhabitants, in particular on children, or rather on a group of children who came quite frequently early in the morning to my small laboratory."

"A random sample?"

"No, actually not quite by chance. Thanks to the support of a priest, Father Angelo, who has lived there for years, I knew that some children already had health problems. Father Angelo knows many families of the landfill well because he has been following them for years. There was a visit from an international health protection agency which ascertained the presence of pathologies in several children. The agency carried out the surveys, but then did not continue its activity. When I arrived to carry out my research as a doctor, Father Angelo asked me to follow the children closely. It would have been very useful for my research, so I contacted Kurt's association, already involved in Agbogbloshie, which helped me to integrate the tools provided to me by the university, in particular for blood sampling and x-rays."

"But how was he able to do the analysis? I mean… it needs a real laboratory, I guess?" Nigel asked.

"That is also thanks to Father Angelo. He had contacted a laboratory in Accra, to which I sent the samples," answered Catherine.

"A decisive and persuasive type, the priest?" Nigel suggested.

"Oh yes! You ought to know him!"

"I still have so many questions I'd like to ask you."

"Please, that's why I'm here, if I can help you."

"For example… did you visit these children every morning?"

"No, not every morning. But with a certain frequency which increased in later weeks. Their blood values were very altered, as was, unfortunately, the state of some of their vital organs. At least a couple of them are really, really sick. But I think Kurt already gave you my report, right?"

"Yes, it is very technical, but I understood the substance. That's what matters. You must have grown very fond of the children?"

"Very, definitely, even if I never had the opportunity to visit them outside of work, as I would have liked." Catherine stared blankly for a moment, absent.

"Was it easy to work over there?"

"No, not at all. Mainly because I was not accepted by most of the inhabitants. The rumour had spread that I was there to close the landfill, and this obviously alarmed those who earn money from it. For this reason, the children were accompanied very early in the morning by Father Angelo, while other people were still sleeping. In this way we avoided creating embarrassment or problems for their families."

"And what did the children think?"

"They thought I was a sorceress, and that everything was a game for their own good. Of course, they didn't understand exactly why they were there. They enjoyed the tools they saw, that I used on their increasingly stressed physiques, even if they didn't realise it. Kids are like that, they think they're always fine. Just give them something to play with and everything smiles for them. It was also enough for them to eat the candies or sweets that I offered them every time I finished my visits, and they began to laugh, forgetting that they had to wake up early to come to me while it was still dark."

"You talk about it with affection."

"Does it seem strange to you? I've been in their lives for five months – from afar, but I've been with them. I know more about their health than their family members. I know the clinical picture of each of them and, unfortunately, I can imagine the next fate of some."

"What does that mean?"

"Many have very serious illnesses, some probably incurable. Besides, it's all written in my report."

"Want to tell me about them, their names, their lives?"

"Why? For your programme?'

"I wouldn't need you for my programme. I could do it equally without knowing the faces and lives of those children who work and play in the landfill. After all, I only have five minutes. What do you want me to say in five minutes? No, it's not for the programme, or rather not just for that; it's more to understand."

"Understand what?"

The waiter arrived with the two coffees and interrupted their conversation for a moment. "Would you like something to go with your coffee? For the Christmas period, our specialty is the chocolate and raisin Christmas scones?" he offered.

"No, thanks, not for me," said Catherine.

"Not for me either, thank you," said Nigel.

The waiter smiled and walked away.

"Understand what, Nigel?" Catherine repeated.

"I don't know. You see, even a few days ago I was talking about it with Kurt. Maybe because it's my first programme of a... let's say 'social' nature. So far, I have only dealt with music, with rock and pop ensembles from the 1960s onwards, of customs and fashions that have followed the various musical eras. My world is that. I have never been particularly fascinated by human and social rights issues, despite having many friends who are activists on this front. I've always been considered noncommittal. And I was also fine with that, all things considered. For me, the main interest was, and still is, to feel good and enjoy all the comforts. If the benefits of industrialisation mean that I enjoy more gas particles in the air that fill my lungs with all the crap... okay, I'll take that into account."

"So, what has changed with this programme?" Catherine was interested.

"That I am not among the injured. If my actions affect those who have nothing to do with my wellbeing, the question changes."

"Wow, a social moral... of guilt?"

"Probably. I didn't know before. Perhaps I can be told that I can't 'not' know. But I do now."

"So, you want to 'know' the lives of some of the little victims of your actions? Don't you think you blame yourself too much?"

"Maybe, who knows? Maybe in a short time I want to make up for years of total extraneousness to the real world."

"You're not alone. Many of us live far from the dramas of life for the majority of the time; and it's hard to notice, in a world that rewards only power, fame, success, wealth. Without realising it, we have slipped into a nihilism that makes us privilege image over substance. Excuse me, I don't mean to be pessimistic; I'm not. It's probably because I still feel the experience of those kids' lives strong in me."

Catherine broke off. She picked up the cup of coffee she had almost forgotten and poured in two spoonsful of sugar, which she stirred slowly. "You see, Nigel, I don't know how to help you. I could tell you what I experienced, but not let you hear their voices, their breath, their coughing, smell the scent of their skin.

But I knew you would ask me something similar. Kurt told me yesterday about your eagerness to know more."

"Really? Did Kurt mention it to you?" Nigel asked.

"Yes, Kurt told me about your drink" – Catherine smiled – "and so I thought I'd bring you something. Two gifts arrived from Accra. One is a notebook, a sort of diary in which Father Angelo collected and recounted the last few days of my stay in the village – or rather the lives in those days of the boys I treated. I would have liked to know more, but it was precisely for their sake that I stayed away. Once, I told Father Angelo about it while we were having tea. I may have given him the same impression that you are giving me: the desire, and perhaps also the presumption, of wanting to enter the heart of people's existence."

"Yes, it's like that for me too." Nigel nodded.

"Anyway," Catherine continued, "a few days ago, immediately after my arrival in London, I received a letter and this notebook from Father Angelo. I made a photocopy, thinking that reading these pages could be more useful than my story." She handed a package to Nigel and then continued: "I'm a university researcher, and that world had to be researched. I came back with a bag full of writings, medical analyses, scientific results. But those pages are not, and never will be anything true in my life. These are the papers of Father Angelo. Perhaps they will help you find the difference between a programme, like many others, and one that enters the life of those who listen to it."

After so much data, and so many testimonies, now Nigel had faces and names. He had people. As with other aspects of his life, he had reality, without adjectives.

"Thank you, Catherine, I'll read it all right away," he said, calmly.

"Take it slowly, over a nice cup of tea," said Catherine

smiling. "You savour every word and try to think of yourself there with these guys."

"I will do it."

"Good. Now I have to go. But first be aware that it hurts to consider yourself disinterested in the society in which you live. You know, all the children featured in the pages of this diary love music, and some have favourite songs, songs that mean something to them. Music always has a story, and it tells that story to those who listen to it: the life behind a song, the society that surrounds a singer or band. A singer may never have been an activist for peace and justice in the world, but that doesn't mean he's insensitive or estranged from the world around him."

They went out into the cold of the street.

"Uhh, looks like winter has arrived. For a woman who comes from Africa, it must be quite a leap," said Nigel.

"Yeah, and not just because of the cold," Catherine agreed.

"Thank you, Catherine, for everything. I wish you happy holidays. Maybe one day we will meet again."

"Why not? Happy holidays to you too, Nigel."

The two set off in different directions, when suddenly Nigel turned. Catherine was still close enough to be called without too much shouting.

"Catherine!" The woman turned. "I forgot to ask you one last thing: what was the second gift?"

Catherine opened the padded leather briefcase and showed him its contents. "The best recycled gift I could ever receive!"

The two looked at each other and laughed together.

Agbogbloshie, November 29

That day, after school, the boys did not go to the dump, and instead, they gathered at Nelson's uncle's warehouse to finish the gift for the sorceress. They wanted to take it to her that same evening, defying the ban on revealing that they visited her. They knew she was leaving early the next day, and they knew their mothers wouldn't wake them up this time. That warehouse had become the site of another secret, at least according to them. There were no dreams there, no daydreaming; there was concrete work and a common project.

They understood that the sorceress had tried to help the Roses of Agbogbloshie bloom, had tried to defeat the junkyard. More or less consciously, they began to understand that she was not the enemy, but one day she would disappear from their lives.

They didn't give up on the promises born there; everyone kept their dreams. But they began to have a common dream. They had never talked about it, but even the book that Father Angelo sometimes leafed through with them had another meaning now. It was called 'Memories from Italy' and it was a collection of photos, with just a few lines, in a language they didn't know, written under each picture. Expanses of blue sea in which cliffs covered with an intense green were reflected by the water; forests nestled beneath mountains gleaming white, with something Father Angelo called 'snow' which claimed to be water, only a little colder; and then there were colossal buildings, often clearly in ruins, but which never looked like the waste that formed the strange mountains of the landfill.

Now for the children, they were no longer just images, photographs. They were new questions. They were beginning to wonder if they could one day see those buildings and those landscapes in real life, where there was no rubbish but harmonious lines, and where the intense colours were not cancelled by the fumes of the landfill fires. And they were starting to think that the situation in Agbogbloshie could get better too. After all, even the junkyard had given them something beautiful and important, the gift for the sorceress.

"We should wrap it well," Ama suggested, while Palletta cleaned the keyboard and Nelson checked that all the pieces were in order.

"We have to check something more important first," she said.

Kofi corrected her, "We forgot something."

"It's all right. We fixed the keyboard and the mouse wheel and polished everything," Nelson reassured him.

"But have we checked if it works?"

"It already worked when I found it. And then we tried it last time too, remember? We just had to fix a few pieces," Nelson said.

"Let's double-check now. Let's turn it on and see."

"We can't; my uncle hasn't bought electricity for the warehouse for two days."

"Let's go to the Centre. There is light there."

They knew where to get it. In front of the statue of Our Lady, in the large room that served as a church and school, there was a light bulb that was turned on every night. Father Angelo had given up on electricity in his room but had wanted to be sure that there should never be a lack of light for anyone wishing to spend a few moments in prayer.

Nelson reached for the power cord behind the statue and unplugged it.

"Maybe we should ask permission," Ama said.

"Of whom? Father Angelo and the nuns have not yet returned from their rounds at this time," replied Palletta.

Ama insisted, "We have to ask permission for it from the Madonna! The light is hers, and we are taking it away from her."

"But how do you ask permission from a statue?"

"It's not just a statue. She will understand. Father Angelo always tells us that she understands because she is a mother, and we can ask her everything. Let's ask her."

Kofi smiled at his little sister and looked at the statue: "Our little Madonna, forgive us but we need your light for a few minutes. As you know, we have prepared a gift for the sorceress; you know her name and perhaps it was you who sent her to us."

"Don't change the subject; let's hurry," Nel said.

"We need your power because we fixed this computer but we don't know if it works. I know we should have checked earlier, but we just thought about it now. And now we have only a little time to give it to the sorceress. I promise you we'll only use a little current. And while you're at it, please make the computer work, otherwise we won't know what to give her. Thank you," Kofi finished.

Palletta and Ama had approached the statue. The children touched the decorations on the pedestal.

"We are your roses like these here. Help us,"

"Yes, help us," the boy repeated.

"Help us," all the others chorused.

Nelson took the plug from the computer and plugged it into the socket. A small light came on in the display.

"It lit up!" Ama exclaimed softly. "But it's all black!"

"Wait." Nelson moved the mouse and a small white arrow, and a drawing of a circle with a line inside appeared on the screen. He moved his hand again and brought the arrow to the drawing. He pressed a mouse button and the screen lit up.

"It works, it works!"

"Try writing something, Nelson," Nii suggested.

Nelson put his fingers on the keyboard, on the letters 'a' and 'v' that hadn't worked a few days ago, then erased them and typed more.

"It's incredible! I've never seen anything like it. But how does it do it? Is it magic?" asked Osagyefo again.

They lived in the middle of all that stuff in the landfill, but mostly the little ones had never seen a complete one of those objects they collected for work. And even Nii, who had once accompanied his father to the city, where there was a computer in the hotel lobby, hadn't been able to see it turned on.

"What did you write?" asked Osagyefo, who still couldn't read well.

The older boys said in chorus: "Our little Madonna, the Roses of Agbogbloshie thank you."

"Yes, thank you, now we give you back the light you lent us!" guaranteed Osagyefo.

Father Angelo, who had witnessed the interlude unseen, stayed hidden.

They hurried back to the warehouse. They searched in vain for some paper to wrap the computer. Then they stuffed it into a cloth bag, ragged and with holes in it, that Nelson's uncle had tossed in the junk corner.

"It's not very beautiful," one child said.

"It'll be fine," reassured another.

Their voices chased each other in their haste to conclude. But Ama had found a piece of paper and an old pen.

"Let's write down our names," she suggested.

"But I can't spell it," Osagyefo replied.

"I'll help you. I'll write it here on the floor and then you copy it onto the sheet," Palletta told him.

"Write Aziz's name, too," Ama suggested.

And off they went, holding hands, even though there was no need to because it wasn't dark anymore. Kofi was leading them, a little surprised that no one seemed to be paying attention to them.

They went down that road, which for five months had meant them losing so many hours of sleep. But now they no longer remembered the lost sleep. They just knew that they had become better friends on those pre-dawn walks, eating together in that house with milk and biscuits. Nobody knew exactly what had happened, or why. But the sorceress had always been good to them. Each time she used a strange contraption to sense how they breathed. And with that she had allowed everyone to feel how their hearts were beating. Little Osagyefo knew from the first time that it didn't hurt when she tied a rubber band tightly around his arm and then pricked it with a needle to draw some blood.

Only Kofi was now sure he knew why the sorceress had arrived a few months ago. He had listened to the speeches of the grown-ups and knew that many did not like her. And he remembered when five months earlier Father Angelo had come to his house to talk to his parents. He hadn't understood what they were saying, but his father's voice was angry or perhaps frightened, the mother's uncertain but also frightened; and the voice of the priest, quiet but insistent.

The next day, Abenà had waited for her husband to return

from fishing. She had made him a cup of hot drink with the precious leaves of that tea preserved in a jar that was used only on special occasions, and then she had said to him: "If it's for the good of the children, it's right to do it." And the man had limited himself to embracing her without answering.

From the next morning, Kofi's mother had started waking them up early to send them with Father Angelo and the other children to the sorceress. And within five months, the Roses of Agbogbloshie had begun to unfold.

They had always arrived just before daylight. This time they were at the sorceress' door just before dark.

"Pull the bell chain, Kofi," Nelson said.

"Yes, then we'll run away immediately," Nii intervened.

"Why do we have to run? I want to say hello again!" Osagyefo replied.

"No, Osagyefo, it's too late. We have to go home and then… I'm ashamed," Palletta answered.

"About what?" Ama asked. "We have done nothing wrong! We're giving her a gift."

He couldn't explain to her any shame, other than the one it feels like to do something wrong. He couldn't even explain it to himself.

But Kofi also had felt something similar. "Nii is right. Let's ring and run away immediately."

Nelson set the briefcase and the sheet of paper in front of the door, Kofi pulled hard on the chain, and everyone started running. But the door opened immediately, and the sorceress saw them. She looked younger without her white dress, wearing just a pair of jeans and a t-shirt.

"Children, are you okay? Has something happened?" She took a step and bumped into the package in front of the door. She looked at the children who had stopped a few yards away.

They wanted to tell her that this was a gift, and she wanted to run and hug them tighter than she ever did. But they all fell silent and only smiled. The children waved their hands to her again and then ran on.

The sorceress picked up the bag, saw what it contained, and said silently: "Thank you, children. Until we meet again." And maybe for once it was true.

London, December 11

"Good morning to all of you, my dear friends. I'm Nigel Tornton, but today, I'm not going to talk to you about music, my first and eternal passion. You should know that a few days ago my boss summoned me. I was terribly afraid that he would want to fire me, and instead he said to me: 'Nigel, from now on your space will have to talk not only about music but also about current affairs, politics and society.'

"Me? Talking about all this? I know. Don't say anything, because I thought so too. But the boss is the boss and work is work. So I took hold of my first programme on a topic other than music, and I've decided to tell you about it in my own way, as a story that we live every day is told.

"You know when you go these days, all out of breath and stressed out, to buy a nice computer or a trendy mobile phone as a gift for your children, your wife, your girlfriend or maybe even for yourself? Well, you buy it and you are happy with it for a few months or a few years. Then, at the first sign of a scratch, or as soon as a new, more up-to-date product comes out, you think about changing it and throwing it away.

"Have you ever wondered what happens to it? You might throw it in a bin, if you are not diligent, or in one of the spaces provided for the collection of electronic material, and the problem is over for you.

"But not for others. All this stuff is collected in large containers that are taken from our ports by sea to African ports, to be piled up in huge landfills. One of these is in Agbogbloshie, on the outskirts of Accra, the capital of Ghana. It's a neighbourhood, indeed a city that grew up on our electronic garbage. Tens of thousands of people sleep, eat and live near millions of tools and electronic devices, piled up where once there were meadows, fields, rivers and which are now all destroyed, polluted and harmful to health.

"Ironically, the landfill can also be a source of income for those poor unfortunates who live around it, often their only source of income. Because that's where they go to collect metals, for example, the copper of electric wires, to resell. And to do all this, they must first burn the plastic around those metals. Now imagine that fumes and poisonous gases rise into the sky to be inhaled by adults and children of your children's age, particles land on their skin, penetrate their organs and slowly destroy them. And the same particles cover the earth, making it barren and poisonous. All this is happening now, while I'm talking to you, and maybe while you're on the way to buy yet another computer.

"Whose fault is this? A chain of powers and interests that we small and helpless citizens can't even imagine! This is why I'm inviting you to read a report. It's called *Economy for Human Rights* and it comes out today. Look for it on the internet or in the newspapers. I'm a journalist and I have to tell you about this.

"Society is not just made up of numbers or words. This is why I am now leaving aside conventions, international agreements and figures. They are important though, so please go and read the report.

"Now imagine the faces of a group of children who live and work in the landfill and who don't even know that I, this radio and all of you, exist. Call them, if you will, the Roses of

Agbogbloshie. Every day they are in contact with that polluting material, they breathe that polluted air from the fumes of the bonfires in which the cables and housings are burned to extract the copper. They get sick and die from it. But don't think of them as sad and indistinct beings. They are real, like our children; they have dreams and would like to make them come true. They don't live on Mars, far from us, but on our own planet which we are destroying in our eagerness to have more, in the illusion of being a little better off.

"Here is your Nigel Tornton, wishing you a good day with a track I want to dedicate to the Roses of Agbogbloshie: *Life on Mars* by David Bowie."

Outside the window, Mike, who came out of his office, as soon as he realised that Nigel had totally disregarded his instructions, looked at him and gave him the okay sign.

Agbogbloshie, December 3

Dear Catherine,

I hope your return journey has gone well and that you have had the opportunity to rest for a few days before resuming your work.

Since you left, the kids keep asking me about you, where you are now, and if they'll ever get a chance to see you again, above all, Aziz, who's now in hospital in Accra due to the worsening of his condition. It goes without saying that they are very fond of you, and I am sure that the memory of the hours spent together will always remain with them.

On the other hand, I'm not sure that they have yet understood the reasons for our meetings. I think they consider them a sort of mystery, as if a superior and magical being had chosen them, among other children, because they have special qualities. After all, they call you 'the sorceress'. I confess that I'd rather agree to their illusion than tell them the truth. And then, isn't this also true? Special they are, even if not for the reasons they would like, and they need special attention. Therefore, I admit my little sin of silence is continuing even now, after your departure, to avoid telling them about the real reasons for our meetings.

In recent months I have been very close to these children. I have observed their movements, listened to their speeches, intuited their thoughts. I certainly didn't want to steal the job from their guardian angel, but partly because of my name, partly *because of my role, and above all because of my love for them, I have tried to be as close as possible to these little creatures, praying for them. I remembered something you said to me during one of the breaks we managed to take over a cup of tea, that is, that you would have liked to be close to those children even outside the work, and that you were sorry to have had to stay away so as not to embarrass them and their families. So I thought I'd write the story of our little friends, at least during the last few days you were in Agbogbloshie.*

I would have liked to give you this diary when you left, but the photos of the children you will find there were missing at that point. I didn't get to print them until yesterday.

There is a photo with Aziz in the centre wearing my old Napoli shirt with its Number 10 – Maradona's. I took this picture after the annual game between the two boys' teams, a game that Aziz was unable to play because his condition had worsened. But his comrades still wanted to associate him with the victory. I thought that in this way, their faces and their memory could accompany you in the future days of your life.

With great affection,
Father Angelo

London, December 13

Dear Father Angelo,

I have just received your letter. Let me tell you right away that the news of Aziz's cancer getting worse caused me pain and a sense of bewilderment, even if, unfortunately, it didn't surprise me. After all, I visited him for five months, did his blood tests and measured his values.

I gave him medicines to at least alleviate the conditions caused by the progress of the disease, those which I then left behind, almost in the hope that a miracle could intervene and that your little baby, as you call all your children, could recover. I was absolutely aware of his state of health and that he could no longer bear the poisonings that had destroyed his respiratory tract. I knew everything, and yet I was unable, as soon as I heard the news, to hold onto that barrier between my feelings and real events which I have always forced myself to keep when a patient of mine has no more hope. I only hope that the response from the doctors at the Accra hospital will leave Aziz some time to be without severe suffering with his family and friends.

For me, Aziz and the others were no longer just patients, a university study or a scientific report. During what you call our breaks, I listened with interest to all the stories you told me about the children: their stories, their aspirations, their dreams, their quarrels.

I too would have liked to be present in each of those moments you told me about, to see their smiles and their looks as they absorbed everything that goes on around them, to be able to hug them when they were happy and even more when they were bitter. But as you know, I didn't want to create tension nor did I want to set myself up as a protagonist in a world that I was only observing and in which I could not, and did not want to, intervene. I couldn't, as you do every day, spend my heart and life among those people, without making promises but still feeding a spark of hope.

I confess that I was also uncomfortable. And not just because of the friction my presence could generate but because of something deeper. Because I know that the dump is there, and will always be, because it is convenient for too many. And I know that my work, yet another denunciation in yet another report, will lead to no change for those people. Do I still feel the same way? Unfortunately, yes, as far as the landfill is concerned. But I have changed my opinion about my behaviours. If I could go back now, in those months I would not remain secluded in my laboratory but would carry out my work asking for hospitality in your Centre.

I understand now, only now, that my real fear was that I was unable to take any responsibility for this world. I don't want to describe this as worse than it is. My dream, like little Nelson's, was to live on Mars. Remember when I used to sing along with Nelson as I drew his blood? It was my favourite and had become Nelson's favourite. But while for him, Mars represents a new world to discover, for me it represented a refuge. I too wanted to imagine a life away from reality, but to escape from it.

I had a job to do, pathologies to study. For five months I forced myself to be just an observer, a researcher. But it is life *that really imposes itself, not us. And I watched our babies and, little by little, I learned to love them. I watched Ama's shy expressions when she asked me what the Prince of England was like, believing that I knew him. I saw Kofi's dreamy eyes when he talked about the journey he would make when he grew up to reach his favourite team, or those eager plans of Kwame who had already imagined his whole business with candy.*

And I saw them again, I relived them in the photos and in the diary you sent me, the best gift you could give me. I read and reread it and at every line I smiled and suffered. You will excuse me if I gave a copy to a journalist who was to report on African landfills. He had news of data and facts, but he knew nothing of the humanity that exists around that landfill. I was sure you would agree to let the stories of the Agbogbloshie Roses be known to those who want to know the reality, not just to make a sterile denunciation. And believe me, that reporter wanted to know the souls that populate Agbogbloshie, not be a mere reporter. We cannot remain merely observers in this world, even if fear or indolence or selfishness often lead us to be so.

And while I sang Life on Mars with Nelson, you taught all the Volta children the back list of your favourite singer, Fabrizio De André. I've learned to love him too, and not just for that song. It's strange how music accompanies our lives, how our feelings are covered by a symphony of song or suite notes.

What will I do now? I will continue to look at Mars, but no longer as a refuge from the world, rather as a pass to overcome to meet the new. I really hope I can do something for those kids. Maybe work there again. Maybe just to see them again.

But I'll tell you what I will do now. I will come out of my university laboratory room, and I'll put on headphones and listen to the Fabrizio De André CD that you gave me when you greeted me at the airport. It's a sunny morning here and the university avenue is bathed in a beautiful winter light. I'll walk to the exit as I've done thousands of times over the last few years, but this time I'll do it while listening to his song, Volta la Carta. Outside there is the road, the deafening noise of engines, the throng of women, men and children frantically going about their duties. And I will mix with them.

Yours,
Catherine Miller

TO KNOW MORE

(2014, October 24) 'Final destination landfill. The London model', *Adnkronos*.

Levine, D. (2001, January 5) 'Toxic Memo', *Harvard Magazine*.

DesJardins, J. R. (2001) *Environmental Ethics: An Introduction to Environmental Philosophy*. Translated by S. Iovino. Toronto: Wadsworth-Thomson Learning, p. 232-233.

Attanasio A. and Giorgi D. (2015, April 13) 'Agbogbloshie, how to live in the largest electronic waste dump in Africa', *L'Espresso*.

(2015, April 24) 'Where the computer goes to die: the landfills of our electronic waste that poison Africa', *Corriere della Sera*.

Scialò L. (2012, April 6) 'Scandalous! Africa is used as a landfill for hazardous waste and electronics', *Tuttogreen*.

The Summers memo at
https://en.m.wikipedia.org/wiki/Summers_memo